SEEKING JUSTICE

L. A. DOBBS

CHAPTER ONE

A chill ran down Police Chief Sam Mason's spine as he took in the grim scene before him. Amidst the towering trees of the owl sanctuary, a woman lay sprawled on the ground, her face obscured by a curtain of blond hair. Next to her, the lifeless body of a tiny owl, its white feathers ruffling in the breeze, tugged at Sam's heartstrings.

The hush of the forest felt heavier, the usual ambient rustle of leaves and chirping of distant birds eerily absent. The only sounds piercing the quiet were the restless sniffing of his K-9, Lucy, and Beryl Thorne's intermittent nose blowing.

His second in command, Jo Harris, methodically documented the scene. With phone camera in hand

and razor-sharp focus, she made a record of the crime scene.

"Did you see anyone leaving?" Sam's voice cut through the silence, his eyes meeting Beryl's. Always a little too close for comfort, Beryl stood near him, her red-rimmed eyes peering out from a crumpled tissue.

"No." Beryl sniffled. "I came to photograph the owls, like I usually do, and then... I found her." She leaned into Sam, her sobs soaking the fabric of his uniform. Sam caught Jo's gaze over Beryl's trembling form. Jo rolled her eyes. Lucy let out a low woof as if agreeing with Jo's eye roll.

"Beryl," Sam said, gently extricating himself from her grasp. "You can head home. We may need more from you later, so be ready."

"Thanks." Beryl managed a half smile, her doe-like eyes shimmering with unshed tears. She turned and left, her body trembling slightly. The vulnerability in her posture tugged at Sam, but an instinctive caution held him back. He watched her leave, a familiar unease niggling at his conscience.

His gaze flicked back to the crime scene, but his mind drifted to Beryl's notorious husband. Lucas Thorne, the underhanded swindler and suspected drug dealer, had been a literal thorn in his side for years. It was Beryl's evidence that had finally put the man behind bars, yet her eagerness to betray her own husband raised more questions than it answered. It was true that she did come to photograph the owls often, but Sam still got a feeling that might not be the whole story.

Sam shook off the thoughts. He needed to focus on the scene in front of him.

"Sam." Jo motioned him over. She was crouching by the victim, her fingers lightly brushing away some debris from the woman's hair. Jo's sharp green eyes were narrowed in concentration.

"Look at this." She gestured at the victim's matted hair, revealing bits of bark embedded in the blond strands. "She didn't fall here accidentally. She was hit with that log." Jo pointed at a hefty piece of wood nearby, its rough bark mirroring the fragments in the victim's hair. "Must have been hit hard, too, to fall so hard onto that jagged rock."

Jo moved to a patch of mud near the log, her eyes catching a peculiar pattern. She knelt down, her fingers hovering over the impressions in the soft soil.

"Sam, look at these footprints," she said, her voice laced with intrigue. "The edges have tread, but the middle is smooth. Maybe someone with an odd gait. I've never seen wear like this."

Sam peered over her shoulder. There were three

larger prints mixed among some partials of smaller ones. "Me either."

He turned to take in the scene. The soil underneath the leaves on the ground was muddy. Because of the layer of leaves, there weren't too many footprints. He could see Beryl's near the body and a few where she had been standing. The other smaller ones had probably been made by the victim.

The leaves partially covered up another thing, the gun which lay near the body. "There's the gun," Sam pointed out.

Jo snapped a few pictures. "What kind of killer leaves the gun?"

"Good question." Sam dialed the medical examiner as Jo continued to survey the crime scene, her eyes darting between the lifeless woman and the fallen owl. The sunlight filtered through the trees, casting dappled patterns on the forest floor. A soft breeze rustled the leaves overhead. It would have been almost pleasant if not for the circumstances.

"Look at this." Jo lifted the owl's wing carefully.

Sam looked down to see a bullet hole right in the poor bird's chest, out near the wing. His gaze was riveted to the body. No bullet holes, at least not that he could see. "We should call John. I need to get a better look to see if our victim was shot too."

Jo looked disgusted. "Who would shoot an innocent owl?"

Sam gestured to the body. "Same person that would murder, I guess." Sam's gaze swept the area. "I don't see the bullet though."

"Maybe we can get Wyatt out with a metal detector."

"Good idea. Let's be careful not to disturb those footprints. We can take a cast of them."

Sam turned his attention back to the victim, whose long hair obscured her face. As he gently pushed the strands aside, recognition flickered through him. Blood seeped from a wound on her forehead, evidence of a violent meeting with the jagged rock beneath her. "I know who this is."

Jo, who was crouched next to him, glanced at him curiously. "Who is she?"

He let out a sigh, his eyes never leaving the lifeless face. "April Summers, the environmental activist."

Recognition flashed in Jo's green eyes. "The same one who chained herself to a tree in the logging area?"

"That's the one." Sam's mind was racing. "Had quite the fallout with the owner of the logging company, Travis Burton. I had to intervene."

Jo's left brow quirked up. "Well, then looks like we might already have our first suspect."

Their attention was diverted by Lucy's urgent barking. She was a few yards into the woods, her body stiff and alert, tail wagging slowly. Sam and Jo hurried over to her, crunching leaves underfoot.

Lucy's intelligent amber eyes were fixed on a splash of color among the fallen leaves—a bandana, its red-and-black design contrasting with blotches of neon-green and hot-pink paint. Jo took a few photos and then picked it up with gloved hands and slid it into an evidence bag.

Holding up the bag, Jo gave Sam a meaningful look. "And now we just might also have our first clue."

CHAPTER TWO

S am and Jo left the medical examiner and his assistants to examine the body and rushed back to the police station.

They found their receptionist, Reese Hordon, standing in front of the desk. Her black hair was tucked under a White Rock Police Department baseball cap, and she had a paint stick in her hand.

"Rocky Bluffs or Quail Egg?" Reese asked.

"Huh?" Sam blinked, trying to decipher her question.

Reese stepped aside to reveal two cans of paint sitting on the desk. Major, the station's resident black cat, was perched atop one can, his luminescent green eyes narrowed as he watched Lucy trot over. Sam braced himself for some hissing and clawing, but the two animals simply sniffed and then ignored each other. Maybe they really had come to some sort of truce.

"Gray or beige?" Jo clarified, nodding toward the paint cans. She paused for a moment, scanning the worn walls. "I vote gray."

"What's wrong with it the way it is?" Sam liked the way the station looked. It was like stepping into the past. The scent of aged paper and stale coffee lingered in the air. Embossed brass post office boxes, still bearing the proud image of an eagle, served as a makeshift divider between the reception area and the bullpen. The old metal desks, with their history of nicks and dents, were scattered haphazardly across the worn wooden floor. Sam glanced at the scratches on the floor near the coffee machine, each one a silent testament to past arrests. He smiled, remembering how one particularly stubborn thief had left the long, jagged line next to the filing cabinet.

Reese wrinkled her nose. "We need to jazz it up. Add some local artwork maybe. The walls, they're just... grubby."

He looked back at Reese then at the cans of paint. With a noncommittal shrug, he said, "Okay. Whatever Jo said."

Sam headed past the post office boxes to the

bullpen. Kevin Deckard was seated behind one of the desks, diligently focused on a stack of paperwork.

Lucy bounded over to Kevin, her tail wagging high in the air. Kevin dropped what he was doing to pet her, a large smile playing on his lips. The two shared an unspoken bond, born from the night Kevin took a bullet meant for Lucy. That same bullet had thrown Kevin into a coma, and although he was back now, it was only part-time until he fully recovered.

"How you feeling, Kev?" Sam asked, casting a side-long glance at the man.

Kevin's smile broadened, though it didn't quite reach his eyes. "Pretty good. Doc says I might be able to come back full-time very soon."

Something in Kevin's tone had Sam pausing. Was Kevin covering up something? Was the healing not as smooth as they all hoped? He decided to let it pass, for now.

"You brought donuts!" Jo snatched the white bag from her favorite coffee shop, Brewed Awakening, from Kevin's desk and headed to the coffee machine. "Coffees?"

Everyone wanted one. Major hopped up onto the filing cabinet to supervise as Jo worked the K-cup machine, pouring her own into a yellow smiley mug last.

"So what about the case? It was murder? Who was it?" Reese leaned against the wall and sipped from a blue mug. She'd taken the call from a distraught Beryl, so she already knew there had been a body found at the owl sanctuary.

"April Summers," Sam started, pulling out a maple-frosted donut and taking a bite. "A conservation activist."

Reese raised her eyebrows, accepting a sugar-dusted donut from Jo. "The one who chained herself to the tree at the logging site? I've heard she's made a lot of enemies."

"That's her," Sam confirmed, washing down his bite with a sip of black coffee.

Kevin looked up from his cinnamon twist, confusion etching his brows. "She was found at the owl sanctuary, right? Wyatt took the Crown Vic up there with the metal detector."

"Right," Jo chimed in, pouring cream into her coffee. "But the most baffling part is the dead owl lying next to her."

Kevin's brow furrowed in confusion. "You mean to say the owl was also... murdered?" he asked, his grip tightening on his donut.

"In a way, yes," Sam replied. "It was shot."

"But the woman, April, she wasn't?" Reese asked,

moving to lean against a desk, her coffee cradled in both hands.

Sam shook his head. "Doesn't seem so. We found a log near the body, bits of its bark caught in her hair. We think she was hit with it, fell, and hit her head on a rock."

Kevin sat back in his chair, nibbling on his cinnamon twist, eyes narrowed. "That's odd. If the killer had a gun, why resort to a log?"

"Anybody home?" A voice rang out from the reception area, and Reese poked her head around the post office boxes and motioned someone to join them. It was Jackson Pressler, one of the older residents of White Rock. Sam wasn't surprised to see him. Jackson had been the one to discover the rare owls on his property and petition the government to make that area a sanctuary. He must have seen all the activity.

"Hey, Jackson, what can we do for you?" Sam asked.

Jackson ran his hands through his white hair, nodding grimly. "Saw the cars heading up the dirt road to the sanctuary. Can't help but worry."

Jo, ever the empathetic soul, wheeled a chair toward him. "Have a seat, Jackson."

Jackson waved it away, standing resolute. "Don't

need it, thank you, Jo. I just need to know what's happening near my land."

Sam met his gaze, deciding honesty was the best approach. "There's been a murder, Jackson. At the sanctuary."

The old man's eyes widened, shock and anger flashing through them. "Again? Damn it! I've said it before, and I'll say it again. It's that Thorne construction stirring up trouble." He jabbed a finger into the air for emphasis. "Saw a young fella trespassing the other day while I was out fishing on the Hogback River behind my place."

"Did you recognize him?" Sam asked, already mentally making space for another suspect on his list.

Jackson shrugged. "Eyes aren't what they used to be, and he was far away. But he was young, wore a black-and-tan baseball cap. Hightailed it out of there when he saw me."

Sam nodded, and Jackson continued. "Hate to think there's a killer running around."

Sam returned Jackson's gaze, a solid resolution hardening in his own. "Jackson, I assure you, we're on it," he said, giving the man's shoulder a reassuring squeeze. "This isn't a random act, and we already have a lead to follow up on."

"Who was it?" Jackson inquired, curiosity lighting up his eyes.

Sam pursed his lips, thinking for a moment. "Can't say yet," he finally responded, casting a glance toward Jo, who was already settled at her desk by the window, laptop open. "We need to notify the next of kin first."

"I'm on it," Jo confirmed, her fingers flying across the keyboard.

Sam's gaze returned to Jackson. "Suffice to say, it's someone who might have ruffled a few feathers."

Relief washed over Jackson's face, the tension in his shoulders easing. "I appreciate that, Sam."

With a final nod, Jackson turned and made his exit from the station. As the door closed behind him, Sam redirected his attention back to his team. "Guess I better get going and interview our first suspect."

CHAPTER THREE

Kevin watched Sam, Jo, and Lucy leave the station. He felt a twinge of longing. He was dying to get back out in the field, but he'd have to convince the doctors he was ready for that first.

Turning his back on the door, he stepped toward the metal filing cabinets. His part-time duty was to file that paperwork, a job he'd done dozens of times before his accident. He knew the system like the back of his hand. Or he used to. Right now, he just stood staring at the cabinets, uncertainty furrowing his brow. The cabinets seemed like uncharted territory. He stood before them, an unfamiliar sense of disconnect gnawing at him.

How hard could it be? They probably filed them alphabetically. He was sure he'd remember the system once he opened the drawers. He had to figure it out either way because he didn't want anyone to know there were still gaps in his memory. But the way Jo had looked at him oddly made him think she might have guessed.

The station door creaked open, pulling Kevin out of his thoughts. He couldn't see who it was from his position, but a knot of worry formed in his stomach at the thought that Sam and Jo might have returned. He turned to the filing cabinet, feigning nonchalance as he opened a drawer.

A voice wafted over to him, the tone as smooth as a polished river stone. "Hey, Reese, brought you some brownies for helping me out."

"You didn't have to do that," Reese said.

"That's what friends are for. So, they're really letting you paint this place?" the smooth voice said.

"Yeah, it needs it."

Kevin couldn't see them, but he imagined Reese gesturing toward the gray paint. What was the color? Rocky Bluffs. A beat of satisfaction pulsed within Kevin. He'd remembered the color of the paint, a small-but-significant sign his memory was still healing.

"You can say that again. Oh! Hi, Major."

Kevin almost shouted out a warning to the woman with the smooth voice, but then the sound of a familiar meow echoed through the room, followed by the sight of a black streak of fur darting past the PO boxes. A woman in a sunflower dress followed quickly behind. With an ease that spoke of familiarity, she swooped down to scoop up Major. Few managed that feat— Major was notoriously aloof.

As she straightened, her gaze found Kevin's. Her eyes, wide and inquisitive, met his, and for a moment, everything else faded away. There was a hint of recognition, a spark of curiosity, and in the pit of his stomach, Kevin felt a flutter of something he couldn't quite name.

"Oh. Hi," the woman said as she cradled the cat. Major's fluffy tail swished in the air. "Kevin, right?"

"That's right." Kevin's brows knitted in curiosity. Who was this cheerful woman?

With a graceful motion, she released the cat, who landed sprightly on all fours, shaking himself off before stalking away. As Major disappeared around a corner, he shot a glance back at Kevin. An unspoken "I'm not always as grumpy as I seem."

The woman extended a hand, her voice warm and bright. "Bridget, Jo's sister."

Jo's sister? Kevin allowed himself a moment of surprise before he gripped her hand firmly, her introduction giving him a sense of familiarity amidst the whirl of changes. She seemed so unlike Jo, who was all business and plain outfits. Bridget, in contrast, appeared free-spirited and whimsical in her sunflower dress and tousled dark hair. "Pleasure to meet you."

Bridget's eyes roved the room, a small frown creasing her forehead. "Is Jo around?"

"She's out with Sam... and Lucy," Kevin added quickly, noting her fondness for animals. Anyone who appreciated animals was all right in his book.

"Can I assist you with something?" he asked, hoping to extend his hospitality.

"No, I just came to chat with Jo," Bridget replied, her gaze drifting from the paperwork in his hand to the filing cabinet. "Those go in the bottom drawer, don't they?"

Kevin blinked, taken aback. "Um..."

Bridget gestured at the folders he held, her cheeks flushing slightly. "Case files. I've seen Jo file them numerous times."

"Oh, right," Kevin stammered, scrambling to cover his confusion. "I was just... just sorting out the paperwork."

Bridget studied him for a moment, her gaze insightful. His pulse quickened. Was she piecing together his struggle? Yet something in her eyes communicated understanding, not judgment.

"Are you just visiting?" he ventured, trying to shift the attention away from himself. He hadn't even known Jo had a sister.

"No." Bridget shook her head, her hazel eyes meeting his. "I'm living with Jo now."

"Oh." For a second, panic gripped him. Had he been expected to know that?

Noticing his discomfort, Bridget's expression softened. "A lot happened while you were in the hospital. I'm here to stay now, though. It's a long story."

"Ah, right. Well, it's great to meet you, Bridget."

"Likewise." Bridget beamed, her positivity contagious. "Well, I'd better get going. It's nice to meet you, Kevin, and I'm glad to see you're doing well enough to be back to work." With a final wave, she made her exit, leaving Kevin with the echo of her laughter and a newfound sense of belonging.

CHAPTER FOUR

"**K**evin seemed a bit off, didn't he?" Jo broke the comfortable silence in the White Rock Police Department Tahoe, her eyes trained on the winding road ahead. Lucy's head popped between the front seats, a soft whimper escaping her. It was almost as if she were joining in on the conversation.

"You noticed that too?" he asked.

"Occupational hazard," Jo responded with a quick smile, her eyes sparkling with a hint of mischief. "Always observing."

Her light-hearted jab drew a chuckle from Sam. His eyes, lined with laugh lines that had deepened over their two years of partnership, twinkled. "Guess that's why you're a detective."

"But I hope Kevin is okay," Jo said, her tone

turning serious. She reached back to pet Lucy, the dog's snout pushing against her hand as if echoing her concern.

"Adjusting after a coma takes time. He'll be all right," Sam assured her, turning onto the dirt road that led to the logging site. "Did you dig up anything on April Summers?"

Jo nodded, her eyebrows furrowing in thought. "It's peculiar. She pops up six years ago, making waves as an activist, chaining herself to trees, leading sit-ins at construction sites. But before that, it's like she didn't exist. I'm still looking for any family or next of kin."

"Every person has a past. She must have family, someone we can notify," Sam mused.

"Exactly. No one just pops out of nowhere. I'll keep looking."

As they drove on, the dense forest gave way to a large clearing. Jo's gaze swept over the area, her usual cheery demeanor replaced with a tight-lipped silence. The sight of the bare landscape, a stark contrast to the lush forest, always left a sour taste in her mouth. Yet she understood its necessity and admired the company's effort to maintain a balance, working on one area at a time to allow regrowth. However, the forest's sacrifice reminded her of the stakes of their current case.

The distant buzz of chainsaws signaled their

arrival at the logging site office, stationed in a repurposed trailer. A woman emerged, shielding her eyes from the sun. In her late thirties, she had a hardened look that reflected years of working under the rough conditions of the logging industry. Her posture was tense, a common reaction to unexpected visits from law enforcement.

"Can I help you?" Her voice matched her appearance, gritty but not unkind.

"We'd like to talk to Travis if he's in," Sam replied, his gaze wandering past her into the confines of the trailer.

"He's down the road, overseeing the crew." She pointed in the direction of the cacophony.

"And you are?" Sam probed, maintaining a friendly tone.

The woman's demeanor softened a bit. "Danika Ryder," she said, extending her hand. "Travis's assistant."

Before further introductions could be made, a truck came barreling down the road, dust billowing in its wake. Travis. He clambered out of the truck, concern etched on his weathered face. "Chief, what brings you here?"

Jo studied his demeanor. He did look a bit worried, but was that because he'd murdered someone last night or because he was doing something else he didn't want them to know about?

"Just following up on something," Sam responded, managing to keep his voice level. "A body was found at the owl sanctuary."

"I don't get out to the owl sanctuary. Don't much care about the owls," Travis said.

Lucy, ever the dutiful K-9, sniffed at Travis's feet. He shifted uncomfortably. Jo noted the impression his boot left in the soft ground—a distinctive circular tread pattern.

"Well, you might care about the victim..." Sam began, leaving the sentence hanging for a moment.

"Victim?" Travis's voice took on an anxious edge, his glance flicking toward Danika.

"April Summers. I hear you two didn't exactly see eye to eye," Sam continued, watching Travis closely.

Travis scoffed. "Sure, she was a thorn in my side, shutting down operations for a day. But kill her? No way." He shook his head emphatically. "That woman was trouble. I'm not the only one that she caused trouble for. She cost Archie Wells a bundle over those condos he wants to build over on Pine Street."

Sam frowned. "She did? I wondered why construction stopped over there."

"She had something to do with that, I believe.

You'd have to ask Archie. But if you're going to put everyone she crossed on your suspect list, then it's going to be a pretty long list."

Sam nodded, then his gaze focused on Travis. "So where were you last night?"

"Last night? That's easy. Was here working on the books." He looked at Danika, and she nodded. "During the day, I have to oversee the crew, but I need to keep up with the accounting, so one night a week, I work on them here at the trailer."

"Was anyone else here?" Sam glanced over at Danika, expecting her to chime in, but she just looked down at her feet.

"Nope, sorry. Now I have to get back to work." Travis gestured toward the forest. "Unless you have more questions?"

"Not right now. We'll be in touch when we do." Sam glanced at Danika, and they left.

Sam and Jo climbed back into the Tahoe, the echoes of Travis's protests still hanging in the air along with the lingering scent of freshly cut lumber. Lucy leapt up into her designated spot in the back, tail thumping against the seat.

As they settled in, Jo turned to Sam, her face contemplative. "That boot print Travis made back there didn't match the one at the crime scene."

"Doesn't mean he doesn't own another pair," Sam replied, his gaze focused on the road as they began to pull away from the logging site.

The heavy hum of the Tahoe's engine filled the silence, allowing them a moment to digest the latest revelations. The buzz of Jo's phone shattered the quiet. Glancing at the screen, her face softened at the sight of her sister Bridget's name. Jo and her sister had been working on a cold case that touched them both personally—the unsolved abduction of their other sister, Tammy, when they were children.

Bridget's text flashed on the screen: *Got some new info on the serial killer angle. Will catch up at home later.*

Sam glanced over at Jo, catching the tail end of her text conversation. "Updates from Bridget?"

Jo nodded, stowing her phone away. "She's got something on the cold case. She'll fill me in at home tonight. You in?"

Sam glanced in the rearview mirror at Lucy, who wagged her tail in response. "Wouldn't miss it for the world," he said, his face softening into a determined smile.

CHAPTER FIVE

Lucy stopped short in the police station lobby, where Reese was crouched on the floor with a roll of blue painter's tape in her hand. Jo almost ran into the dog, and Sam almost ran into Jo.

"What are you doing?" Jo asked.

Reese turned to look at them, and Lucy trotted over to sniff her face. Reese crinkled her nose and laughed as she petted Lucy's soft fur. "I'm taping the molding so we get clean lines with the paint."

"Of course, I knew that." Jo was no stranger to painting. She just hadn't expected to see Reese on the floor. Apparently Lucy had felt the same, but satisfied that nothing was wrong, she trotted into the station. Major was not concerned. In fact, he was taking advantage of Reese's absence at the green steel reception desk and was lounging on top of it.

Sam and Jo followed Lucy into the bullpen. Wyatt was engrossed in paperwork at his desk. He looked up, the tattoo ink on his arm visible from under the edge of his rolled-up shirt sleeve.

"How'd it go with Travis?" he asked.

"Says he didn't kill her, of course, but he did mention that April had a few enemies," Sam said.

Wyatt grimaced. "I suppose that's no surprise. Tends to happen when you disrupt businesses."

Jo nodded. "Did you come up with anything?"

A glint appeared in Wyatt's eyes. "Well, it seems the gun was registered to the victim."

Jo's brows shot up. "That is interesting."

"It's wiped clean, though. And she wasn't shot." Wyatt held up the preliminary report from the medical examiner.

"Didn't think so." Sam started toward his office. "Maybe we better go in my office and start organizing the investigation."

"I printed out some of the pictures I took as well as some of Jo's from when you were there this morning." Wyatt handed Sam a stack of paper, and the trio moved into Sam's office with Lucy following closely behind.

Sam made his way behind the vintage wooden table that served as his desk. The old scarred wood of the tabletop was littered with round postal stamps, evidence of its prior life in the post office.

Jo tugged a chair from the corner, its mismatched leg causing it to rock slightly as she settled down.

Wyatt chose to stand, his attention focused on the large corkboard behind the desk as Sam began arranging photographs from the crime scene.

Lucy plopped herself into the warm pool of sunlight that streamed through the tall windows that overlooked the town square.

Sam placed the pictures one by one. April, lying motionless on the ground. The innocent owl, white feathers marred with blood. The gun. The log. The bandana. Various angles of the entire scene.

"I suppose it's too much to ask that Travis was wearing a bandana when you visited him." Wyatt pointed to the picture of the bandana.

"He wasn't," Sam said.

"Maybe that's because he lost it in the woods," Jo chimed in.

"Good point." Sam continued tacking up the last few pictures.

"But we don't know that bandana had anything to do with the murder because we found it a ways away from the scene." Sam turned to Lucy, who was asleep in the sun. "Actually, Lucy found it."

Wyatt nodded. "Must have some meaning then if she brought your attention to it."

Sam tacked up the last picture of a bullet in a branch. It looked a little off-kilter to Jo.

"That photo," she began, head tilted to the side as she pointed at the picture of a bullet nestled in a branch. The angle seemed slightly askew. "You took it from below, looking up, right?"

Wyatt nodded. "Yeah, I figured since the owl was probably in a tree, the bullet might've ended up there."

"Good thinking." Sam glanced over at Jo, and she shrugged. They'd only looked on the ground.

"But are we thinking this was all an accident then?" Jo asked, gesturing from the images of the owl to those of the woman. "She shoots, misses, the bullet hits the branch, and it falls on her?"

"Well, the weird part is that the gun was wiped clean. No prints," Wyatt interjected, pausing for a moment to let the information sink in. "So if she didn't shoot, then who did?"

Jo's brows furrowed in thought. "She wouldn't wipe the gun after an accidental shooting. Unless"— she glanced at the two men—"she was trying to frame someone else? But even that doesn't make much sense."

"But why use her own gun for that?" Sam questioned, crossing his arms.

"And she was hit with a log. The back of her head had traces of bark," Jo added. She gestured to the picture of the log. "That's no accident."

"Someone else had to be there," Sam deduced, studying the images. "Maybe they shot the owl then hit her with the log..."

"But how would they get her gun?" Wyatt asked.

"And why shoot an owl?" Jo added

Sam glanced at Wyatt. "What do we know about April's time in town? Any idea where she was staying?"

Wyatt nodded. "She checked into the Ledgewood Motel. I talked to Bruce Johnson, who owns it, but he won't let me in until I produce a search warrant."

"All right." Sam sighed. "I'll get on that warrant. Meanwhile, Wyatt, dig into any digital trails she might have left. Jo, you keep trying to find anything about her family. There's got to be something out there that will explain more about who would have a motive to kill her."

CHAPTER SIX

Bridget maneuvered her car onto the stone driveway of the cottage she shared with Jo.

The quaint old cottage was always a welcome sight. Nestled in the forest, it was a faded red with white shutters. Flowers spilled from window boxes and planters, a riot of colorful petunias, pansies, and impatiens. It was off the beaten track, quiet except for the babbling of the brook out back and the chirping of birds. It was small but homey.

Orange fur moved on the porch. Pickles, the feral kitten she and Jo had been trying to look after, watched her. His curious eyes were wide and alert. She stepped from the car, slow, calculated. No sudden moves. Pickles was a bolt of lightning when spooked.

She squatted, extending a hand toward Pickles. "No pressure, little guy."

The small cat approached cautiously. He sniffed and then recoiled. Probably smelled Major.

Bridget laughed softly. "Major can be a bit off-putting, but he's really a nice cat."

Pickles looked up at her skeptically. Even though the two cats had never met, there must be something in his scent that warned Pickles that Major was a tough cookie.

Turning her attention to a bowl tucked away in the corner of the porch, she noted it was scraped clean. A satisfied smile tugged at her lips. She'd been leaving food for Pickles, and it seemed to be working. "Good boy, Pickles."

But at her words, the skittish cat darted off into the lush greenery. She watched his retreat, a soft sigh escaping her. Each day brought her a step closer to gaining his trust. By the time winter crept in, maybe Pickles would consider the porch, or even the warmth of the indoors, a safe haven.

Unlocking the door, she stepped inside, greeted by the soothing bubbling of the fish tank. Finn, Jo's pet goldfish, glided around his aquatic home. His golden-orange scales glinted under the tank light, the color as vibrant as a summer sunset. The fish darted up, a well-trained response to the likelihood of a food opportunity.

Bridget retrieved a bright-red flake from the food jar, dangling it just above the water's surface. Finn rose, snapping up the flake in a quick, eager pucker. He then hovered, eyeing her for more treats. With a laugh, she indulged him with a couple more flakes.

"All right, Finn, that's your lot," she said with an amused shake of her head. "I've got everyone else to feed."

A spark of anticipation kindled within her. She had news to share, information about Tammy's disappearance that she'd uncovered. Bridget could hardly wait to share her findings with Sam, Jo, and Holden Joyce, the FBI investigator who had been helping them.

Bridget unpacked her culinary treasures from the local specialty store. Her growing interest in cooking, born from the long hours she now found at her disposal, had led her to explore more gourmet options. She wanted to put together something nice for Jo, Sam, and Holden.

She started by unwrapping the cheeses—a creamy brie that felt like velvet under her fingertips, a sharp aged cheddar with a robust aroma, and a tangy goat cheese, crumbly and soft. She arranged them thoughtfully on the polished wooden board she had recently acquired, its rich grain adding an elegant touch to the presentation.

Next came the crackers—an assortment of whole-grain, seeded, and classic water biscuits, each offering a different texture and flavor profile. Bridget enjoyed the rhythmic sound they made as she placed them strategically around the cheeses, imagining the different combinations her friends might try.

The figs were her personal favorite. She loved their unique, sweet flavor and the way their softness contrasted with the cheese and crackers. She placed them on the board, their deep purple skins adding a pop of color and a hint of exotic flair.

To complete the array, she added some cured meats—thinly sliced prosciutto, spicy salami, and a few slices of smoked ham. Their savory scents mingled with the other elements, creating an inviting aroma.

Jo entered the kitchen just as Bridget carefully positioned the last of the meats on the tray.

"Pretty fancy. Not sure this crowd will appreciate it." Jo folded a slice of prosciutto into her mouth, her eyes sparkling with amusement. "Just regular cheese and crackers would be fine."

Bridget shot her a wry smile, her fingers nimbly arranging a handful of cheddar cubes. "It's fun.

Besides, it's the least I can do." She didn't elaborate on how much Jo's support over the years and her sister letting her live here meant to her.

"Seen Pickles today?" Jo asked, peering through the window, her gaze trailing into the woods.

"Yep. He ate the food I left. Let me pet him, but I don't think he liked smelling Major on me, though."

"Major? The cat at the station?"

"I stopped by to see if you were in when I was in town getting the food. I hope you don't mind." The thought hadn't occurred to her that Jo would mind, but maybe she did?

"Not at all! Sorry I wasn't there." Jo grabbed a cube of cheese then frowned. "Major lets you pet him?"

"Yeah. He's sweet." Bridget, relieved that Jo didn't mind her stopping into the station, artfully arranged grapes on the board. "I met Kevin. He's getting the hang of things, it seems."

"Kevin's been cleared for part-time work." Jo's tone was a mix of relief and concern. "But something doesn't sit right. He puts on a brave face, but I can tell he's struggling."

Bridget kept her focus on the board, rearranging grapes to avoid Jo's penetrating gaze. She'd noticed something off about Kevin, too, but decided to play it down.

The way he'd been looking at that filing cabinet told her he had no idea where to file things, and the way he'd pretended like he knew exactly where the files went told her that he was trying to hide that fact. But the reason he had memory issues was because of the coma he'd been in when saving Lucy from a bullet, so that made him a hero in her book. "I think he was acting fine. He was filing up a storm when I went in."

Jo quirked an eyebrow, her worry easing slightly. "Really? That's a relief."

A sudden knock on their door stole their attention

"Hey, you guys in there?" Sam's voice rang through the small cottage.

"Yes, come in!" Jo yelled.

Seconds later, Lucy burst into the kitchen, all tail wags and wiggles.

Bridget exhaled a sigh of relief. For now, she'd keep her observations about Kevin to herself. After all, everyone had their secrets. Even her.

SAM FOLLOWED Lucy into the kitchen, where Jo and Bridget were preparing food. He raised an eyebrow as he snagged a piece of cheese from the elaborate plate on the kitchen counter. "What's all this? Looks pretty fancy."

Jo chuckled and passed him his favorite Mooseneck beer. "You know, there's a world beyond canned beans and hot dogs, Sam."

"Hi, Sam." Bridget gave Sam a hug, and he felt a beam of pride. He couldn't really take credit for the way Bridget had cleaned up her addiction, but he liked to think he'd helped a little bit.

"I've been watching cooking shows and thought you guys might enjoy some of the finer things in life. There are figs, three kinds of cheeses, and prosciutto." Bridget handed the tray to Sam. "Will you take it into the living room?"

With the beer and plate, Sam moved into the living room, Lucy following closely behind.

Sam eased into an armchair, his gaze roaming the room. The place had a touch of feminine charm that was a far cry from his rugged cabin, but it wasn't frilly, so he didn't feel out of place. It was clean, cozy. Filled with trinkets that gave it a lived-in feel. "Place is looking good, Jo."

Across the room, Jo was arranging a few more logs in the fireplace, her back to him. "Yeah, I'm settling in now, and I've got a meeting with the landlord tomorrow. Try to make it permanent," she said, her voice casual. Too casual.

Sam eyed her for a moment. She was trying to act casual about it, as if it didn't matter, but she wasn't fooling anyone. "Hope you're not paying list price. You put enough work into this place. Brought it back to life."

He took a swig from his beer, eyes flitting back to the fireplace.

"We'll see." Jo finally turned around, a hopeful glimmer in her eyes.

Sam nodded, taking another sip. "Best of luck. You deserve it."

"Thanks, Sam." Her lips curled into a small smile. The kind of smile that said she appreciated his words more than he knew.

All he could do was tip his beer in response, sinking a little deeper into the chair. Even though he and Jo were close, all this time he'd wondered if maybe she was only renting because she didn't plan on staying. He was glad she was making a move to buy the cottage. He'd hate to lose her at the station and as a friend.

A lingering twinge of hurt remained in Sam over Jo's initial secrecy. She'd come to White Rock for a lead on her sister's case, not opening up to him about her true motives until very recently. Yet he understood that situations could spiral and lines could blur. He'd been down that road himself, keeping secrets when perhaps he shouldn't have.

As they talked, the door creaked open, diverting their attention to the entrance.

"Knock, knock." Holden Joyce stood in the doorway with a six-pack of beer. Holden had to be in his early sixties, but the only thing that gave away his age was the gray in his hair.

Sam glanced at him, grudging respect in his eyes. "Look who's here. Old Man Winter himself."

Holden's hearty laugh filled the room. "Flattery will get you everywhere, Sam. Or is it mockery? I can't tell the difference."

Sam shrugged, a wistful smile playing on his lips. "Maybe a bit of both."

Bridget gestured toward an overstuffed chair. "Have a seat. Want a glass for your beer?"

With a simple shake of his head, Holden replied, "Nope," as he twisted off the beer cap and took a leisurely sip. He eased into one of the plush chairs, eyeing the charcuterie board with a slight frown.

Sam noticed and felt a grin tug at the corners of his mouth. Apparently, he wasn't the only one who thought it was a little bit fancy.

Once upon a time, the relationship between Sam and Holden would have been described as rocky at best. But things had changed. Sam knew that Bridget saw Holden as a father figure, and that alone carried weight. And now, with Holden helping them dig into the cold case of Jo and Bridget's sister, Sam found his initial skepticism about the man waning.

As if on cue, Lucy ambled over to Holden, her tail wagging in restrained optimism. She nudged his hand with her nose, and he obliged, petting her softly. Sam watched the interaction, his thoughts crystallizing.

If Lucy liked Holden, then he had to be decent. That dog had instincts sharper than any detective's, and her approval was as good as a background check in Sam's book.

Perhaps it was time to fully let go of past reservations. After all, they were all on the same side now.

Sam scooped up a fig with a cracker. Was that how you were supposed to eat those things? Should he put cheese on it? He added a piece of cheese and took a bite. That was pretty good, so maybe Bridget was on to something.

Bridget leaned in, shifting the atmosphere. "Remember Eve Duchamp?"

Jo nodded. "Our babysitter? She was devastated when Tammy disappeared."

Holden took a sip of his beer before speaking. "The FBI put her family under the microscope, especially her dad."

"He was cleared, though, right?" Jo asked, a trace of old pain in her eyes.

Holden shook his head. "Yep. They found nothing on him. But the scrutiny still left a stain on the family. They changed their name and moved away."

Bridget glanced at Jo. "So, what originally brought you to White Rock?"

"I got a tip from one of the seasoned detectives on Tammy's case," Jo began. "But what does Eve have to do with any of this?"

Bridget piled some prosciutto and fig on a cracker. "Well, you remember she moved away, and as Holden said, her family changed their last name."

Jo, who'd been reaching for another slice of cheese, paused. "Yeah?"

"Turns out they moved to White Rock," Bridget stated, her eyes meeting Jo's.

Jo looked back and forth between Bridget and Holden, her hand hovering in midair. "What? But her family had nothing to do with Tammy's disappearance. Are you sure they moved here?"

"Absolutely." Bridget nodded. "Heard a rumor, so I

L. A. DOBBS

checked it through some resources Reese has access to."

Sam's brow quirked up. He knew Bridget and Reese had become friends, but he didn't realize Bridget had called on her to use her resources.

"Don't worry," Bridget hurried to add. "She doesn't know that we are working a cold case. I said it was about an old friend from a former life. I hope I didn't just get her into trouble."

"Nah. I've asked her to do things off the record for me too." Sam leaned back. "Eve's family probably wanted to move away from it all. But moving here is quite a coincidence. People often move near relatives, though. Could just be that simple. Besides, the police cleared the father. Eve would have been too young, but... did she have an older brother?"

Jo met Sam's eyes as she picked up a slice of cheddar. "She did. Barry. But he was never a suspect."

The room fell silent for a moment, the atmosphere thickening.

Sam took another sip of his beer, placing it on the table. "That's a good find, Bridget. We should look into this further."

Bridget looked puzzled, still holding a cracker. "How?"

Holden leaned forward, catching Sam's eye. "First,

find out how long they stayed in town. Are they still here? Any relatives? Were children abducted from this area while they lived here?"

Jo shook her head while she chewed on a cheddar-topped cracker. "Unlikely. Their last name was Duchamp, and there are no Duchamps around here."

"But relatives could be on the mom's side," Sam pointed out, taking a piece of cheddar from the board. "Different last name."

Holden nodded. "Still, it's a long shot, thinking their move here has anything to do with them being involved. But every angle's worth investigating."

He paused, taking a sip of his own beer. "One thing's for sure—this case is different from most others I've worked on. Typically, serial killers go after adults. Tammy was a child."

Sam looked at Holden then at Jo and Bridget. "Which means we are looking for someone who is a true monster."

CHAPTER SEVEN

The thumb drive clicked into the slot with a sense of finality. Kevin's fingers danced across the keyboard, his brow furrowed in concentration. Access denied. He tried another combination. Denied again. Each attempt was a hope rising and falling in the span of a heartbeat.

He reached for his water, the glass cold against his palm, the sound of his swallow loud in the silent room. His eyes were locked on the screen, the blinking cursor a taunt, the password field a chasm between him and the truth.

Why the heck can't I remember?

He was sure that the drive was some sort of evidence in a case, but why had it been in his possession on the day he was shot? His brother Brian had dropped it off with Kevin's personal effects at the station while he lay unconscious, mind and memories adrift. He didn't remember any visits from Brian while he was in the hospital.

The knowledge that Brian had been the one to bring his personal effects to the station was unsettling for Kevin. They hadn't seen eye to eye on most things, their lives taking divergent paths early on. Brian's path had always skirted the gray areas of legality, his career choices a series of get-rich-quick schemes that never quite panned out.

That Brian had been there, talking to the doctors and nurses on his behalf while Kevin was unconscious, felt out of character. It gnawed at Kevin, this niggling suspicion that Brian's presence wasn't rooted in familial concern. Why now? After all these years of distant, sporadic meetups during obligatory family gatherings, why would Brian suddenly care about him?

Brian had not visited and had only called once since Kevin had woken from the coma. Another fact that proved Brian probably didn't really care. There was an edge to Brian's voice on the call, a probing undertone as he asked about Kevin's recovery—no, not the recovery but specifically about when he'd be back at work, what cases he was on.

What are you up to, Brian?

But that was one mystery that might not be solved. With Brian, one never knew. The thumb drive, though... Well, Kevin hoped he could solve that. It could be important.

When he'd first looked at the drive, he thought it was empty. But after talking to Wyatt, he'd discovered that drives could seem empty if someone really wanted to hide what was on them.

Wyatt hadn't seemed at all suspicious as to why Kevin was asking all the questions. In fact, he seemed glad Kevin was interested in computer forensics, and it had been simple for Kevin to get more ideas from him on how to find out if the drive had data on it without actually telling Wyatt he had a drive.

Kevin still wasn't sure why he didn't want Wyatt to know. With his memory being all messed up, he was operating on instinct.

He'd discovered there was data on the drive, but of course, it had been locked behind a password. He'd been trying to crack that password for weeks now. With each failed attempt to breach the drive's defenses, Kevin's frustration mounted.

Maybe this was all for nothing. Kevin squeezed his eyes shut, trying to remember why he had that thumb drive and how to access it. But somehow in the dark

L. A. DOBBS

recesses he felt like he actually never knew the answers in the first place. He was just keeping the drive because it was somehow important. And if it was that important back before he was shot, it was probably pretty important now.

The drive was but one of the foggy memories that eluded him. There was also something about a corner. He had no idea why that kept tugging at him. He felt it was loosely related to Lucy and Sam but had no idea why. Apparently that was important too. Sam had asked him about it and said he mentioned it when he'd been in a coma.

He turned his thoughts back to the thumb drive. Foggy memories emerged. Tyler Richardson, the officer who was shot last year. Lucas Thorne. Did the drive have something to do with them? The names flickered at the periphery of his consciousness, elusive yet insistent. He inhaled sharply, the air cutting through the fog of uncertainty.

Maybe he should just bring it to the station. He was sure Wyatt could crack into it in no time. But the thumb drive had been found in his pocket, which meant he hadn't turned it over to Sam for a reason. That reason eluded him now.

Better safe than sorry. If he hadn't wanted anyone

to see what was on the drive back then, he might not want them to see it now. Better to get a look at it himself first.

His pulse throbbed in his temples as he put his fingers back on the keys. Try again. Keep trying.

CHAPTER EIGHT

The following morning, Sam and Lucy walked into the station and were immediately hit by the pungent smell of fresh paint. He squinted at the walls, now a shade of gray that was actually kind of pleasant. Reese was wielding a paint roller with an artist's focus.

"Hey, it's looking good, Reese. Smells like a chemical plant, though."

"Beauty often comes at a cost, Sam." Reese set the paint roller down, bent over to pet Lucy, and grinned. "Lucy, stay away from the walls." Reese raised her voice, yelling into the squad room, "You, too, Major, especially that tail of yours!"

Just as Sam was about to reply, the front door burst

open, and in strode Mayor Henley Jamison, his expensive suit impeccably tailored and his tie flapping over his shoulder as if caught in a breeze only he could feel. He halted midstride to sneeze then scowled at the freshly painted walls.

"This does look better," he conceded, nodding at Reese, who was standing paint roller in hand. "Good job."

Sam glanced from Reese to the mayor then asked, "Something I can help you with, Mayor?"

Jamison's frown deepened. "I'm here about that case involving the activist. The owl people are in an uproar."

Sam raised an eyebrow. "Owl people? I didn't know we had owl people."

"Well, we do. They call themselves the Owl Protection Society, and they're on my case," the mayor huffed, striding past the row of brass-embossed post office boxes that doubled as makeshift dividers.

As the mayor and Sam entered the squad room, Jo and Wyatt looked up from their battered metal desks. Jamison's eyes narrowed as he surveyed the room, his expression softening as his gaze settled on Major, who was on top of the metal filing cabinet.

Major, who lashed out at most visitors, had recently taken a liking to the mayor for reasons Sam couldn't understand. The cat rolled on his back and purred as the mayor took something from his pocket.

"Got something for you." Jamison tossed the toy to Major, who batted it from the air with one paw. It landed on the ground, arousing Lucy's curiosity.

Lucy trotted over.

Major jumped from the cabinet.

Lucy sniffed the toy.

"Meow!" Major lashed out his razor-sharp claw, connecting with Lucy's nose.

"Yipe!" Lucy ran off into Sam's office, and Major picked the toy up in his mouth and trotted off in the opposite direction.

"And here I thought they were getting along," Sam said.

"Sorry." Jamison shrugged. "So, back to business. I need this case solved pronto before the news blows up. The owl aspect adds interest and pretty soon it will be on all the TV stations. That won't be good for my campaign."

Sam felt a spike of annoyance. The mayor's political concerns should be the least of anyone's worries when a life was lost. "We're doing everything we can to seek justice for the victim, campaign or no campaign."

His eyes flicked to Jo. "Any progress on identifying more about the victim?"

She shook her head. "Not yet. Still running down leads."

Jamison seemed visibly perturbed. "Well, you better find something fast."

"It would help if you got that search warrant issued so we could get her things at the motel," Sam said.

Jamison gave a curt nod. "My assistant is faxing that over even as we speak."

They all turned to look at the fax machine, which whirred to life.

"Relax," Sam said, exasperated. "One unsolved murder isn't going to ruin your campaign."

"You should hope not," Jamison shot back. "If you think Thorne buying up land was bad, wait until you see what Convale is planning."

Sam's brows furrowed. "Thorne was a drug dealer. Convale is a corporation. How bad could they be?"

Jamison snorted. "You don't want to find out."

"How do you know so much about that, and what does this have to do with your mayoral run?" Sam asked, increasingly perplexed.

"Let's just say Marnie Wilson has tight connections with Convale," Jamison replied. "If she gets in, you might not like the changes coming to this town."

Sam exchanged a quick, wary glance with Jo.

"Listen, don't worry. We have two good leads, and in my experience, as long as you have one lead, it usually snowballs into more," Sam tried to reassure the mayor.

Jamison leaned in closer, his curiosity piqued. "Leads? Like what?"

Sam took a moment before answering. "Well, Jackson Pressler thought he might've seen someone." Sam didn't mention that Jackson's vague description of a young man in a baseball cap wasn't a blockbuster lead.

"And the other?"

"The victim had some friction with Archie Wells."

"Wells, the builder?" Jamison's eyebrows shot up in surprise.

"That's the one."

Jamison looked puzzled. "You think a guy that high up on the social ladder would resort to murder? It's a stretch."

"I've heard Archie has a temper," Sam countered, locking eyes with the mayor.

"A temper is one thing. Murder's another,"

Jamison huffed, glancing at Jo and Wyatt, who had stopped pretending not to listen.

"I agree," Sam conceded, "but it's a lead, and in my line of work, you follow those wherever they take you."

"Do your best. That's all I ask," Jamison said as he exited, a mix of worry and impatience clouding his face.

No sooner had the door swung shut behind him than Jo and Wyatt swiveled in their chairs. "What was all that about Convale?" Jo's brow furrowed.

"Yeah, he seemed like he was holding something back," Wyatt chimed in, his eyes narrowing.

Sam shrugged, trying to dispel the lingering unease. "What could it be? They're buying up land, sure, which isn't great for us, but how much damage could they really do?"

"But Marnie being in with them? What's that about?" Jo pressed, still puzzled.

"Politics," Sam sighed. "Jamison probably doesn't want any factor, no matter how small, tipping the scales in Marnie's favor."

"But what he said about Convale changing things... That didn't sit well with you either, did it?" Wyatt observed.

Sam paused. "No, it didn't. But how much can

they change? It's probably nothing to worry about, and right now we have a case to solve, so let's make sure Major didn't do any damage to Lucy and then head on out to Archie Wells's place and see what he has to say."

59

CHAPTER NINE

Sam, Jo, and Lucy approached Archie Wells's building, its sleek, modern façade sharply contrasting with the surrounding quaint New England architecture. Sam couldn't help but think it was as out of place as a skyscraper in a cornfield.

As they entered the spacious, well-lit reception area, the receptionist looked up, her gaze flicking from Sam and Jo to the imposing figure of Lucy by their side. There was a moment of hesitation in her eyes, a subtle mix of surprise and concern, before she regained her composure.

"Good morning," she greeted, offering a practiced smile that didn't quite reach her eyes. "How can I assist you today?"

"We're here to see Mr. Wells," Sam said,

displaying his badge. "Chief Sam Mason and Sergeant Jo Harris from White Rock PD."

The receptionist's nod was quick, a little too quick. "Of course, Chief Mason, Sergeant Harris," she said, picking up the phone with slightly trembling hands. "Please, have a seat. I'll see if Mr. Wells is available."

Sam and Jo took a seat in the sleek chairs lining the wall, the polished chrome and leather clashing with the traditional attire of the town's residents. Lucy, unfazed by the surroundings, sat obediently at Sam's feet, her eyes scanning the room.

A few minutes passed, filled with an awkward silence punctuated only by the soft clicks of the receptionist's keyboard and the distant hum of office machinery. Finally, the receptionist hung up the phone and stood up, her posture rigid.

"Mr. Wells will see you now," she announced, her voice still maintaining that rehearsed warmth but with an undercurrent of nervousness. "Please, follow me."

They were led down a corridor lined with abstract paintings, the kind that looked expensive but said little. As they approached Archie's office, Sam noticed the receptionist's pace slowed slightly, her shoulders tensed as if bracing for something.

The office door opened to reveal a spacious room with a large, imposing desk. Behind it sat Archie Wells, a man whose appearance was as sharp as the building he occupied.

Wells was a man who knew how to command a room. Tall and impeccably dressed, he wore a suit that probably cost more than what some people in town earned in a month. His brown eyes had a penetrating quality, like they could dissect your thoughts if you held his gaze for too long. Charismatic but not someone you'd want to underestimate.

He rose from behind his large, imposing desk, a monument to his ego or success—Sam wasn't sure which. Archie offered his hand with a genial smile, first to Sam then to Jo. He moved to greet Lucy next, but the dog stayed put beside Sam, unyielding. Archie's hand hung in the air for a moment before retreating, a brief flicker of annoyance crossing his features.

"What can I do for you, Chief Mason?" Archie finally asked, resettling into his leather chair.

Sam glanced at Jo. She was scrutinizing Archie, her eyes almost squinting. She had that look—the one she got when she was mentally recording every detail. She would have her opinions, sure as day follows night, but for now, she stayed silent, and so did Lucy.

The dog's stillness wasn't lost on Sam. Lucy had a keen sense about people, and her nonreaction was, in itself, telling. Archie might have the charm, the looks, and even the money, but Lucy wasn't buying it, and that was good enough for Sam.

Sam looked at Archie and leaned forward slightly. "We'd like to ask some questions about April Summers."

Archie's jaw tightened ever so slightly. He leaned back in his chair, his eyes narrowing just a fraction. It was a game of minute gestures now, and Sam was all in. "I don't really know her," he admitted. "Just that she likes to get into other people's business."

"Like yours?" Sam probed.

Archie shifted uncomfortably in his seat. "I guess you could say that."

"I heard she was disputing something about the land you wanted to build your latest project on," Sam continued.

"That's right," Archie confirmed. "Said it should be unbuildable as it was wetlands. She was wrong."

"But it held up your project?" Sam pressed.

Archie nodded, his gesture restrained but conveying a world of frustration. "Yes."

"That probably cost you a lot of money," Sam mused.

Archie snorted. "You don't know the half of it.

What's she done now? I hope someone is finally realizing what a fraud she is."

Sam found the comment interesting. "Really? Why do you say that?"

Archie locked eyes with Sam, and for a moment, it felt like a measuring contest. "Let's just say people like her have a knack for making noise but not much else. All talk, no substance. That woman is not what she seems. Why are you asking all this? Something happened, didn't it?"

Sam nodded, watching Archie's reaction closely. "Yeah, April Summers was murdered."

Archie's expression changed as realization dawned. "You don't think I had something to do with it?"

"Did you?" Sam returned evenly. "She was costing you a lot of money."

Archie shook his head. "Was. Past tense. We resolved our issue. But if someone killed her, you might have a long list of suspects."

"How so?" Sam asked.

Archie looked uneasy as he spoke. "Look, I guess it's okay to say this now, but you didn't hear it from me. When I said April was a fraud, I meant it. Sure, she acted like she was gung ho about the environment, but she wasn't above looking the other way if you paid her off."

"Is that what happened with you?" Sam asked, leaning in a bit.

Archie sighed. "That's water under the bridge now, but you can bet if she was trying to extort money from me that I wasn't the only one."

"SO WHAT DID you make of Archie?" Sam asked Jo once they were in the Tahoe and driving away.

Jo turned her gaze away from the window to look at Sam. "I felt like he was really surprised to find out April was dead."

Sam nodded, processing her input. "Yeah, he seemed genuinely taken aback. That part felt real." He paused for a moment then asked, "Do you think he was telling the truth about April extorting money from him?"

Jo considered for a moment before responding. "He seemed to be truthful about that too. His reaction didn't come across as rehearsed or deceptive."

"That's what's puzzling," Sam said, his brow furrowing. "It's out of character for an activist, isn't it?

If she truly cared about the environment, how could she just let people off the hook because they pay her?"

"Maybe she cared more about the money than the environment," Jo suggested. "It's not unheard of for people to start off with good intentions and then get swayed by financial incentives. Could be April was playing both sides."

Sam nodded. "Guess we'll have to dig deep into her financials. You want a coffee?"

"Of course. Why do you even ask?" Jo smiled.

Sam turned into the drive-through of Brewed Awakening, their favorite coffee shop. Lucy's ears perked up in expectation of a donut hole or two.

"If what Archie says about him having resolved his issues with April is true, then he has no motive."

"Well, much as I don't like him, I do have to admit that the apartment complex is under construction again, so maybe he was telling the truth," Jo said.

Sam shrugged. "Maybe. Doesn't mean he didn't have another project that April was trying to mess up. I'll check on that."

They got to the window, and Sam ordered their coffees.

Shelly leaned out the window to smile at Lucy. "You want a couple of donut holes?" She glanced at

Sam for approval, and he nodded. He could hear Lucy's tail thumping against the back seat.

"Here you go, Chief, Jo. Some for Lucy too."

"Thanks, Shelly," Sam replied, taking the bag and handing over the payment.

As he drove away, Lucy let out a soft whine from the back seat, her keen nose having already detected the smell of the donut holes. Jo reached in, twisting around in her seat to offer a donut hole to the dog, who accepted it gratefully.

"So, did you find anything in April's past that might indicate she was into extortion or blackmail?" he asked, resuming their earlier conversation.

"That's the thing," Jo said, sipping her coffee. "I can't find much about her past at all. She's squeaky clean until about six years ago. Then there were the usual arrests that come with being an environmental activist. Before that, nothing."

He took a sip of his coffee, savoring the earthy brew. He hoped it would kick-start his brain into figuring out their next step. "That's strange. Maybe she wasn't into activism before that."

"Or extortion," Jo added. Sam wondered about his next steps. Extortion was a seedy business, the hallmarks of which couldn't often be found through proper police channels. Luckily, Sam knew someone who specialized in digging up dirt like that. Mick Gervasi, his best friend since childhood, was always the guy to call when he needed to go off the record. Mick had a knack for finding out things no one else could.

"Should we bring Mick into this?" Sam asked, his eyes meeting Jo's for a moment.

Sam couldn't see Jo's eyes behind her Oakley sunglasses, but her slight nod and the twitch of the corners of her lips told him she was on board. "He could be useful."

"Wanna meet tonight at Holy Spirits?" Sam asked. Holy Spirits was their favorite bar, a decommissioned church transformed into a local watering hole. "Mick's in town, and I'm sure he'll be up for it."

Jo's eyes twinkled as she chuckled. "Sounds good. Maybe our case will get some divine intervention."

Sam laughed. "Speaking of cases, did Bridget say anything about her plan to look into that babysitter's family?"

"I think she might be talking to Reese about it," Jo responded, her voice tinged with something he couldn't quite place. Hope, maybe? Or fear.

"Maybe we could invite Bridget to join us tonight, discuss what she's found," Jo said.

For a moment, Sam hesitated. Bridget was a recovering drug addict and alcoholic. "You sure that's a good idea, considering it's a bar?"

"It's her choice to make, Sam. If she's uncomfortable, she'll say so."

That settled it. "All right then. We should see if Holden wants to meet up too."

Jo glanced at the dashboard clock. "I have that meeting with my landlord at two, but I'll call Bridget to see if she wants to come, and then she can call Holden. I'll let you know what they said when I get back to the station. Shouldn't be more than an hour or so."

"Perfect. Then we can leave right from the station to Holy Spirits." Sam glanced over at her. "Your landlord's Garvin McDaniels, right?"

Jo nodded.

Sam chuckled. "Be careful with Garvin. My dad knew him, and he's a tough customer. He's gruff around the edges but a softy inside. Still, he won't let that property go cheap."

Jo smiled, finishing her coffee. "I'll keep that in mind."

CHAPTER TEN

Jo's car crunched over the gravel driveway, stirring a cloud of dust as she approached Garvin McDaniels's farmhouse. The old building stood isolated among several acres of unkempt land, its once-vibrant paint dulled and peeling, giving the structure a forlorn appearance. Weeds had claimed the garden, and the fence surrounding the property was in disrepair, with some posts leaning at odd angles.

She parked and stepped out, her gaze sweeping over the sprawling property. Despite its state of neglect, there was a sense of enduring resilience about the place. Trees dotted the landscape, a stone wall edged one side of the property, and wildflowers grew in a field.

Approaching the house, Jo's footsteps echoed on

the rickety wooden porch. She raised her hand and knocked gently on the weathered wooden door, its paint chipped and faded from years of neglect. After a moment, the door creaked open, and Garvin McDaniels appeared on the threshold. His brows knitted together as he squinted at her, taking a few seconds longer than she was comfortable with to recognize her.

"Ah, it's you," he finally said, his eyes still narrowed suspiciously. "Jo, right? You're rentin' the cottage by the creek."

"Yes, that's right," she confirmed, her voice laced with polite formality.

"Something wrong with it? Plumbing's not acting up again, is it?" His voice was tinged with concern.

"No, no, everything's fine," Jo assured him quickly, not wanting him to get the wrong idea. "May I come in? I wanted to discuss something about the cottage."

At her assurance, the tension in Garvin's face eased a fraction. "Ah, all right then. Come on in."

She stepped inside, immediately confronted by a strange sight—stacks of empty plastic yogurt containers piled haphazardly throughout the room.

"Excuse the mess," he grumbled, catching her gaze. "I don't like throwin' things away. Those containers are good for leftovers, though I don't have much of that since Ethel passed."

Jo nodded, her eyes darting around. The clutter and piles of unidentifiable junk gave credence to his statement—Garvin really didn't like throwing anything away.

Garvin shuffled toward a cluttered kitchen counter, brushing aside a stack of newspapers to reveal a sleeve of crackers and a jar of peanut butter. "I'd offer you something, but this is about all I've got," he said, gesturing toward the humble spread.

Jo felt a pang of concern. "You've got to eat more than just crackers and peanut butter, Mr. McDaniels."

His eyes narrowed, taking on a defensive edge. "Ethel used to cook proper meals," he said gruffly, referencing his late wife. "But now that it's just me, why bother?"

Jo sensed she'd crossed a line and quickly tried to reroute the conversation. "I didn't mean any offense," she said. "Actually, you don't have to go to any trouble. I didn't come here for food. I came to talk about the cottage."

Garvin's eyes flicked up, as if caught off guard. "The cottage? What about it?"

"I'd like to buy it," Jo said, her voice steady despite the inner churn of thoughts about Garvin's living condition and the newly added layer of complexity about the property.

Garvin stared at her for a moment, as if processing what she'd just said. Then his eyes narrowed even more. "Well, now, that is strange."

"Why is that?" Jo asked, leaning in, intrigued and confused.

"Because Marnie Wilson was here the other day asking about that very property," he divulged, scratching his stubbled chin.

Confusion swirled in Jo's mind. Marnie Wilson? Why would she be interested in the cottage? Could Garvin be mistaken? She couldn't dismiss the thought that maybe, just maybe, the old man was going senile.

"Are you sure it was Marnie?" she pressed, seeking clarity.

"As sure as I'm standin' here," he asserted, clear eyes meeting hers.

Garvin's eyes narrowed as he considered her question. "Why Marnie Wilson would want that cottage, I couldn't say. But I do know that property is valuable, and I'm not sure I'm ready to let it go."

Jo nodded, respecting his sentiments. "I understand, Mr. McDaniels. But if you ever do decide to sell, I hope you'll consider me. I've poured a lot into making that cottage my home."

He looked around his own cluttered living space, where the weight of memories and collected odds and ends pressed against the walls. "You know, it's not all about money," he said softly, his voice tinged with nostalgia.

"I agree," Jo said earnestly. "For me, it's about the home I've created there. I don't even know the property's worth, to be honest. But it's invaluable to me."

Garvin met her gaze, his eyes softening a touch. "Well, I can appreciate that sentiment. I'll think on it, but as I said, I'm not ready to sell just yet."

"I respect that," Jo said. As she turned toward the door, an idea sprang to mind. The piles of yogurt containers, the crackers, and the peanut butter—all signs of a man missing home-cooked meals and, perhaps, companionship. "If you don't mind, Mr. McDaniels, maybe I could stop by sometime with some baked goods. My sister makes a mean pie."

His eyes brightened for a moment. "I wouldn't say no to that."

Jo smiled as she left Garvin's house. If apple pie and occasional company made him more inclined to sell the property to her, so be it. One thing was for sure —Marnie Wilson was not likely to engage in such a grassroots campaign. Sometimes, the little things did count for more.

CHAPTER ELEVEN

Bridget was perusing the shelves at a cute local cooking shop called Gourmet Haven when her phone pinged. It was Jo.

"I sort of volunteered you to make a pie," Jo said.

"What?" Bridget frowned as she turned down the center aisle. She was on the hunt for saffron threads. She had stumbled upon a recipe for a decadent saffron risotto on the internet and the dish looked too good not to try.

"I just came from Garvin McDaniels's place, and he doesn't want to sell. But all he had were crackers and peanut butter, and his eyes lit up when I mentioned pie, so I figure I can try to worm my way into his good graces with pie."

Bridget chuckled. "If it helps you get closer to owning that cottage, then consider that pie baked. I'm living there, too, after all. But hopefully, not for long. I really want to find my own place."

"No rush on that. I love having you with me."

"I know, but sooner or later, it will be time for me to fly on my own." Bridget loved living with her sister, but the place was small, and it wouldn't be long before they started getting in each other's way. Jo's house was a great place to get on her feet again, but she didn't want to ruin their close relationship by overstaying her welcome.

"Before I let you go, do you want to meet up with Sam, Mick, and me at Holy Spirits around five thirty?" Jo asked.

Bridget brightened at the mention of Holy Spirits. "Sounds like fun."

"You sure?" Jo's voice was tinged with concern. "It is a bar, after all."

Bridget sighed. "You don't have to baby me, Jo. Alcohol was never my thing. Don't worry, I'm not about to spiral."

Jo let out a relieved breath. "I didn't think so. Just double-checking. Oh, and can you touch base with Holden? Invite him too. We can talk more about

Tammy's case. Have you made any progress on finding out more about Eve's family?"

"Not yet," Bridget admitted, "but I might have something to discuss tonight."

"Okay, great. See you tonight."

"Sounds like a plan." Bridget snagged the jar of saffron and headed toward the register.

Purchase in hand, Bridget exited into the sunny day. She was meeting Reese at the local diner and was excited to see what the other girl had dug up on Eve Duchamp and her family.

Bridget walked down the street, her thoughts drifting to the pie. Apple was probably best. Or maybe she should bake a few different kinds and let Jo decide. She was already savoring the wafting aroma that would fill the kitchen, the crispness of the crust, and the gooey sweetness of the filling, when suddenly her thoughts were shattered. A sensation crept up her spine, an old intuition she hadn't felt in years. When she lived on the streets, this gut feeling had been her guardian angel. Her heart tightened. Her breathing felt like dragging air through a narrow straw.

Turning, she caught sight of a man—a tall figure all in black, a figure strikingly similar to someone from her past. Panic surged through her veins like hot lead.

Without another thought, she darted into the nearest alley, back flush against its rough, brick walls. She clenched her fists and waited for him to find her. Each second felt like a lifetime, but minutes passed, and nobody came.

Slowly, Bridget peeked out from her hiding spot. The street had returned to its normal bustle of tourists and locals. Had she imagined him? Maybe her mind had conjured up a monster from fragments of her past. She so hoped that was the case because that man knew things—terrible things she never wanted to resurface.

Taking a steadying breath, she resumed her walk toward the diner. Her eyes darted in her peripheral vision, her heart still thudding like a drum in her chest. She would have to act normal, especially when she saw Reese. No one could know about the man or the dark secrets clinging to her past. She couldn't risk anything ruining the idyllic life she was making for herself here in White Rock.

By the time Bridget reached the cozy, retro-themed diner, her heart had finally settled down, and she felt more like herself. The homey atmosphere of the diner helped calm her down even more. The air was filled with the comforting aroma of coffee and grilled beef. The clatter of dishes and silverware melded with snippets of conversations mixed with laughter from nearby tables.

She spotted Reese already seated in one of the booths, her dark hair pulled back into a ponytail, engrossed in her phone. Bridget felt a momentary burst of gratitude. Making new friends hadn't been easy, and she appreciated the budding friendship with Reese.

"Hey there," Bridget greeted, her voice tinged with genuine warmth.

Reese looked up, and her face broke into a smile. "Bridget! Hey, come sit."

Bridget slid in the opposite side. The red vinyl of the booth was worn but welcoming to the touch, and the lighting—a mix of natural daylight and fluorescent lamps—cast a warm, slightly nostalgic glow over everything.

Bridget felt a sense of relief wash over her. Everything here was normal, homey, easy. No one was bursting through the door trying to ruin her life. Now she was certain she had imagined the man on the street being the same one from her past. Probably just a touch of PTSD from the horrible life she used to lead.

Being around Reese was easy—she was funny, smart, and one of those people who made you feel like you'd known them forever. Bridget found herself admiring Reese, especially her ambition. Reese was going to the police academy, and Bridget couldn't help but feel a pang of envy. What a decisive path to have.

Bridget's eyes flicked briefly over the laminated menu, its colorful pictures of milkshakes and burgers a bit faded from years of use. She already knew what she craved—a comforting grilled-cheese sandwich.

The waitress, a middle-aged woman with a warm smile and streaks of silver in her hair, approached their booth. Her name tag read Jenny, and her uniform bore a few faint stains from what was likely a long shift. "What can I get you ladies?"

"I'll have a grilled cheese, please," Bridget said, handing the menu back to Jenny.

"And I'll take a BLT," Reese added, setting her phone face down beside her coffee mug.

"Coming right up," Jenny assured them, tucking her notepad into her apron and sauntering back toward the kitchen.

"What's in the bag?" Reese gestured toward the small paper bag that sat next to Bridget on the booth.

"Saffron." Bridget grinned, pulling the tiny jar from the bag to show her. "I found a recipe for saffron risotto I wanted to try."

"Sounds delish. I love how you keep trying new recipes and everything comes out awesome. I burn everything I make."

Bridget laughed, the sound tinged with a lightness that belied the morning's unsettling episode. "I'm sure you're not that bad. Besides, you're probably good at a lot of things that I stink at."

Reese's eyes sparkled as she leaned closer over the table. The atmosphere seemed to shift, filling with a sense of expectancy. "Speaking of things I'm good at, I scoured my resources and found out more about Eve Duchamp and her family."

Bridget's heart jumped in her chest. "Go on," Bridget urged, her eyes locked on to Reese's.

"They changed their name to Woodson and stayed in town for years," Reese said.

The waitress came back with their lunches, and they refrained from talking until she was well out of earshot.

"Are they still in town?" Bridget asked.

Reese grabbed the ketchup and smacked the bottom as she poured a puddle for her fries. "Hard to know. I couldn't get any information on that. I dug around a bit but couldn't find out anything more."

Bridget settled back in her seat. "Well, what you did find is huge. Thank you so much. I just hope you're not getting yourself in any trouble for me."

"Don't worry about that," Reese reassured her with a small wave of her hand. "I'm happy to help. Besides, what you're doing—searching for your past, for the truth—it's brave. I admire that."

Bridget felt a warm glow at Reese's words. She needed that encouragement more than she cared to admit.

As they dug into their lunches, the conversation pivoted from the serious to the mundane. Reese entertained Bridget with amusing anecdotes about her police academy classmates and their trainers. Bridget found herself laughing genuinely, her grilled cheese forgotten momentarily as she relished the natural camaraderie.

It had been such a long time since she'd had a friend she could just talk to. A long time since she didn't have to glance over her shoulder, anticipating trouble. And it had certainly been a long time since she could sit down and enjoy a good meal without the weight of her past threatening to spoil it.

A warmth washed over her. Here she was, building a new life piece by piece. A life filled with potential friendships, promising opportunities, and a freedom she had never thought she'd experience. She was determined to protect this fledgling happiness at all costs.

If that man was in town, he couldn't be allowed to talk. Never. Her darkest secret had to stay buried.

Desperation had driven her to unspeakable acts to survive, and the weight of it was a stone, cold and heavy, in her soul. But as she looked at Reese, her resolve solidified.

She'd protect her new life.

At any cost.

CHAPTER TWELVE

"Where's Reese?" Jo asked as she walked into Sam's office. Sam and Wyatt were standing behind the desk, staring at the corkboard.

"Lunch," Sam said without turning around.

Jo's gaze fell on the puddle of sunlight under the window. "And Lucy?"

Sam turned and looked at the place on the floor where Lucy would normally be lying. He frowned. "Not sure."

Sam turned back to the corkboard and the crime scene photos, notes, and maps. The lone footprint was the centerpiece of his scrutiny—a singular trail of evidence that seemed out of place.

"Boots," he muttered, more to himself than to Jo or Wyatt. "Heavy-duty. Not Wells's style. He wouldn't be caught dead in them. And he doesn't have any new projects going for April to mess with, so he might have been telling the truth."

Jo tilted her head, absorbing the implication. Sam was right. She couldn't picture Wells wearing boots. Of course, there were hundreds of people in White Rock who did. But the strange tread could help them narrow down suspects. She pushed off from the doorframe, drawn into the puzzle.

Sam's finger tapped the dirt-impressed sole printed on the photograph. "These footprints definitely indicate one person," he stated firmly. The singular set of tracks emerging from the scene was isolated, indicative of a lone perpetrator—a detail that both narrowed and broadened their scope of inquiry.

Wyatt piped up, shuffling through his notes. "Checked the other set against April's shoes. They're a match." His voice was steady, the facts falling into place like pieces of a familiar puzzle.

"Good work," Sam said.

"And I got the pair of shoes Beryl Thorne was wearing that day." Wyatt smirked. "She asked about you and seemed hurt that you didn't come out yourself."

Jo rolled her eyes.

Sam ignored them both. "And they checked out?"

"Yep, exact match."

"Okay, so we can rule out these." Sam took a red pen and x'd out several footprints. "All that is left is the shoe with the odd tread."

"So we're looking at the killer's footsteps," Jo concluded, the weight of the evidence settling in the room like dust after a scuffle. The theory turned to certainty with her words, sharpening the focus of their quest. "Looks big. Probably a man."

Sam leaned in, his eyes narrowing. "We can determine shoe size, maybe even the make, if we're lucky. If we match the treads to a suspect..." He let the possibility hang in the air, tantalizingly within reach but just as elusive.

"But we need a suspect first," Jo added, the reality of their predicament grounding her speculation. "Can't exactly start flipping people over and checking their shoes."

Sam's attention moved to the photo of the paint-stained bandana. "And this," he said, his voice gaining an edge, "is another clue that might help, but we need to narrow things down to someone painting."

"And let's not forget that Jackson saw a young man with a baseball cap," Wyatt added. "Yet another part of the puzzle. But we need to snap the pieces together."

"Construction workers," Jo pondered aloud, taking

a step closer. "New projects, renovations around town." She was already compiling a mental list of recent building permits issued in the area. "Could just be someone painting their room. Hard to find out who is doing that."

"Might not be a bad idea to talk to Mel down at the paint store."

Before Jo could answer, a ball of black fur streaked through the room. Major carried the toy Jamison had given him in his mouth. Lucy chased behind, her nails scrabbling out from under her as she tried to turn the corner too fast.

"Guess those two are back at it," Wyatt said as they all peeked out into the squad room. Major was up on the filling cabinet, the toy tucked securely under her front paws as he stared down at Lucy. Lucy danced and whined and looked at Sam and Jo as if they were going to intercede for her.

"Sorry, buddy." Sam patted Lucy on top of her head. "I'm not messing with Major, and if you're smart, you won't either."

Wyatt laughed. "Truth. Speaking of messing with the king of the filing cabinet, do you know where the Deardorff file is, Jo?"

"It should be in the bottom drawer," Jo responded,

motioning with a casual flick of her wrist toward the cabinet. The ongoing goat saga between Nettie Deardorff and Rita Hoelscher was town lore by now—comical, if not a tiresome distraction from serious police work.

Wyatt shook his head. "Nope. I looked."

Jo frowned. They always kept it there, but Kevin was doing the filing now. She rummaged around in the top drawer and found it in the back. "Here it is."

"Thanks." Wyatt took the file to his desk. "I need to enter the latest incident. Bitsy ate the giant pumpkin Nettie was growing. Bitsy was Rita's goat, and most of their arguments revolved around her."

"How did it go with Garvin?" Sam asked, shifting gears from the investigative trail to personal matters with an ease that came from years of balancing the professional and the personal.

Jo proceeded to her desk, a half smile touching her lips as she pulled out her bottom drawer and put her feet up on it. "Well, he's an interesting character. Lonely, I'd say. But get this, he said Marnie Wilson was interested in buying the cottage too."

Sam's eyebrows lifted in surprise, mirroring Wyatt's perplexed expression. "Marnie? What interest could she have in your place?" There was a hint of skepticism in his voice.

Wyatt chimed in, "Doesn't add up. Doesn't she live in a fancy house?"

Jo shrugged, the corners of her eyes crinkling in thought. "I'm not sure. Garvin seemed pretty convinced though. But he also made it clear he's not looking to sell just yet."

"You think Garvin was confused?" Sam asked, the detective in him finding it hard to let go of an anomaly.

Jo shook her head, her certainty firm. "No, he was pretty lucid about it. But I have a plan." Her smile turned sly, a hint of mischief sparking in her eyes.

"Oh?" Sam leaned back in his chair, intrigued. "Do tell."

Her smile widened as she pushed off from the doorframe, ready to leave them with something to ponder. "Let's just say I've got a secret weapon to persuade Garvin when he's ready to sell. Homemade pie has a way of opening doors—and persuading hearts."

Sam and Wyatt exchanged a look of amused acknowledgment.

"What? I'll have Bridget make one for you guys too. But right now, I need to get to work on this case." Jo opened her laptop and started typing. "I know there is something on April Summers that will give us a clue, and I aim to find it."

"And I," Wyatt said, "need to meet Bruce at the motel. I got the search warrant, and I can pick up April's things."

"That's good news," Sam said. "Let's hope we find something enlightening."

CHAPTER THIRTEEN

Two hours had ticked by in a blur of fruitless searching when Sam's voice cut through Jo's focus. "Ready to hit Holy Spirits?"

Jo's eyes lingered on the screen for a moment longer before she sighed and stood, stretching the stiffness from her muscles. "Sure."

"I'll just leave Lucy in my office and swing in to get her after we leave the bar."

They often left Lucy alone with some food, and Major lived in the police station, so he had his own food and litter box in a closet.

Jo eyed Major, who still had the toy. He narrowed his gaze at her as if warning her not to take it away. "Let's hope the two of them don't tear the place apart."

Reese poked her head in from the reception area.

"Don't worry. I'll be here for a while, painting. I'll keep them in line."

"Nice job on the paint, Reese," Sam said as they stepped out into the evening, the setting sun casting long shadows on the streets.

Holy Spirits was an easy stroll away, the fading light giving the old church a serene, misleading aura. To the uninformed observer, it was a place of quiet sanctuary, its tall, stately doors suggesting nothing of the revelry within. More than a few tourists had stepped inside, only to be surprised at what was actually in there.

Inside, the transformation from sacred to spirited was complete. The vaulted ceilings created an expansive canvas for hushed conversations and laughter. Dim lighting cast everything in a forgiving amber hue, shadows playing hide and seek in the alcoves.

The rugged charm of the place was undeniable, from the rough-hewn fieldstone walls to the worn wooden floors that told tales of dancing, spills, and the wear of countless boots and heels. A melodic hum from a jukebox somewhere in the background was the heartbeat of the establishment.

In a nod to its past, pews had been repurposed into communal seating, fostering a sense of togetherness among patrons, while the round tables near the entrance offered a more private gathering space. Locals clustered around them, the air occasionally punctuated with the clink of beer mugs and the scrape of chairs.

Jo followed Sam to the back, where the bar stretched out in place of the former altar. The tall windows were a kaleidoscope of jewel-toned glass, setting a sacred backdrop to the rows of bottles that lined the area. The reflected room behind them shimmered in the glass, lending an air of infinite space.

Mick was already at the bar, wearing his trademark black leather jacket and nursing a Scotch on the rocks.

Sam slid into the seat on one side of him and Jo on the other.

"Evening, Sam, Jo," Mick greeted, his voice as smooth as the whiskey he favored.

"Hey, Mick." Sam returned the greeting with an easy nod.

Jo caught Mick's startling blue eyes with her own and gave him a smile.

Before they could dive into conversation, Billie Hanson approached with a practiced smile. "The usual for you two?"

"That'll hit the spot, Billie," Jo confirmed, grateful for the prospect of a cold beer.

As Billie slid the beers in front of Sam and Jo,

Mick tilted his tumbler in request for a refill. Billie obliged with a clink of ice cubes and a swirl of amber liquid.

"So what can I do for you guys?" Mick asked. "I mean, it's good to see you both, but I get the impression you wanted more than a drinking buddy."

Sam laughed and clapped Mick on the back. "You know I always love hanging with you, but as it turns out, we do have a use for your unique skill set."

"You heard about April Summers?" Jo asked.

"The activist?" Mick asked. "Heard she got killed."

"Yep," Sam agreed. "Turns out she was a bit more than an activist."

Mick's eyebrows arched, an unspoken question hanging between them.

Jo turned her barstool to face Mick squarely. "Turns out she wasn't quite the idealist everyone thought she was."

Mick's nod was slow, contemplative. "So you're saying you need someone to do a bit of... unofficial snooping?"

"That's about the size of it," Jo affirmed, taking a pull from her beer.

Their conversation, now edging into delicate territory, was suddenly cut short as Bridget and Holden appeared at Jo's shoulder.

The five of them exchanged greetings, and Billie appeared on the other side of the bar. Bridget ordered a soda water without any hesitation, and Holden did too. Jo wondered if Holden was trying to show support for Bridget.

As they waited, Jo gestured to a corner table, slightly removed from the ebb and flow of patrons. "Let's grab that spot over there. We'll have a bit more privacy for talking."

They all agreed, and once Bridget and Holden had their drinks in hand, the group made its way to the sequestered table. The wooden chairs scraped against the floor as they settled in, the sound muted by the drone of bar noise.

The murmur of the bar seemed to recede as the conversation took a turn toward the serious, the group's collective focus narrowing.

Sam, who had been sipping his beer, set it down with a gentle thud. "What's going on with the case? Were you able to find anything on the babysitter's family?"

Bridget nodded, her eyes reflecting the gravity of the situation. "Yes, a bit of a breakthrough. Their last name was changed to Woodson. And it turns out, they stayed around here for a good while. But that doesn't mean anything. I guess it could be a coincidence."

Mick raised his eyebrows, leaning in, intrigued by the conversation. "Wait a minute. Fill me in on this."

Mick already knew the story about Tammy, so Jo quickly filled him in on the newest information about the babysitter and her family.

Mick rubbed his chin thoughtfully, his gaze distant for a moment as if he were rummaging through an internal archive of faces and names. "You might think it's a dead end," he said finally, "but sometimes all it takes is a fresh pair of eyes. I might be able to help."

"How?" Holden asked, the protective note in his voice softening a bit with curiosity.

Mick's expression was a blend of confidence and mystery. "Well, let's just say I've got a knack for finding people. And I know a thing or two about how folks hide in plain sight. I've seen it happen before."

Sam nodded. "He does."

Jo's brain was whirling. "Wait a minute. How hard is it to change your name?" Jo had never run across that in her investigations to date.

Holden shrugged. "Not too hard. I mean, you have to go to court to do it legally. And then there is a whole process to keep that out of the public records. That's what your babysitter did, so it was hard to find out where they went. Of course, you can't blame them after that notoriety."

"Of course." Jo tapped her finger on her beer. "So then if someone did that, their new identity would appear as if they just came out of nowhere."

Holden nodded.

Jo put her beer down. "Well, that's interesting. Maybe that's why I can't find anything on April Summers."

CHAPTER FOURTEEN

B ridget and Jo turned off their engines in unison, headlights fading to darkness in front of the cottage. The night was still, save for the chorus of crickets and the soft rustle of wind through the trees.

Bridget's gaze swept the shadows that clung to the edges of the porch, half-expecting them to coalesce into the figure of the man from her past. Her muscles tensed, the laughter and warmth of Holy Spirits fading into a cold prickling at the back of her neck. She scanned the perimeter. Every snapped twig or rustle in the underbrush could be him, waiting, watching.

But the night yielded no threats. The only movement was the gentle swaying of branches in the autumn breeze. Pickles, unconcerned with human fears, purred softly, rubbing against her leg. It was enough to loosen the knot of anxiety in her stomach. No one rushed out at her. No ghost from her past appeared.

"Everything okay?" Jo's voice pierced the stillness, her silhouette framed by the doorway.

Bridget's laugh, a little too sharp, too quick, scattered the tension. "Just jumpy, I guess." She dismissed the question, turning to see Jo's brows knitted in concern.

She offered her sister a reassuring smile, a silent plea not to probe further. The last thing Bridget needed was Jo's detective instincts kicking in, unraveling threads best left untouched.

In the shadowed light of the porch, Pickles greeted them with a tentative stare. Bridget was happy to divert the focus to the tiny cat. "Look, he's on the porch."

They approached cautiously, but this time Pickles didn't bolt. He even let them both pet him.

"Wow, this little guy is really making progress," Jo said.

"He is." Bridget checked to make sure Pickles had enough food and water in his little area on the porch then stood and unlocked the door. "He's starting to trust us. Maybe he really will be ready to stay on the porch once it gets cold."

Jo stood and brushed her hands on her jeans. "All the more reason to make sure Garvin sells this place to me."

Bridget, halfway in the house, turned to look at her. "Yeah, with the help of my pies."

Jo grimaced. "I hope you don't mind."

Bridget shook her head. "Not at all," she reassured her. "I love making pies. It's therapeutic."

As they moved into the living room, the ambient light from the fish tank cast a soft glow that seemed to dance across the walls, reflecting the gentle rhythm of life beneath the water's surface. Bubbles meandered upward, and Finn zoomed around, his golden-orange color vibrant under the lights.

He darted to the top as they approached, and Jo sprinkled a few flakes into the tank that Finn gobbled up.

"Tea?" Bridget asked as she headed toward the kitchen.

"I'd love some."

Tea in hand, they sank into the chairs. Bridget blew across the steaming surface of her mug, curiosity alight in her eyes. "So, what did Mr. McDaniels say that had you wanting to give him pies?"

"He's not ready to sell yet, but he seemed like he could use some company. He kept mentioning his late wife, and he barely had anything to eat there. I thought bribing him with pie might be worth a try."

A laugh escaped Bridget, then she leaned forward, her expression turning serious. "And this business with Marnie Wilson wanting to buy it?"

Jo shrugged, the motion loose, nonchalant. "Garvin mentioned she's got her eye on the place. No idea why."

Bridget's distrust was palpable. "I don't really know her well, but something about her rubs me the wrong way."

"Yeah," Jo agreed, her voice dropping a register. "Join the club."

Bridget's gaze held a hint of concern as she hesitated, the mug halfway to her lips. "I hope I didn't land Reese in hot water, you know, with all the dark-web digging."

Jo brushed off the worry with a flick of her wrist. "Not in the slightest. We've tapped Reese's—let's say, unconventional—talents before. I'm kicking myself for not turning to her expertise earlier, actually."

Relief flickered across Bridget's features. "Good to hear. I mean, whatever it takes to figure out what happened to Tammy, right? By the book or not."

"It really gets under your skin, doesn't it?" Jo leaned forward, the case pulling them back in. "That constant gnawing of not knowing what happened to her."

Bridget nodded and took a sip of her tea to distract herself from the hollow feeling she always got when she thought about Tammy.

Suddenly Jo stood and gestured to her sister. "Come on, let's go take a look at what we have. Maybe something will shake out."

In the bedroom, Jo flipped up the corner of the rug and grabbed the old skeleton key that unlocked the antique powder-blue armoire. Unlike any typical armoire, this one was a trove of the unofficial cases that refused to leave Jo's mind. Tammy's case was front and center.

The interior was an array of tacked-up notes and photographs. Together, Jo and Bridget stood before it, reviewing evidence that spoke of darker days—the beech trees with their odd broken and bark-stripped branches, the yellowed clippings from newspapers that had long since faded from memory, and the names of various suspects, all crossed out as they proved to be dead ends.

They both stood in front of it in silence, studying the clues and information, hoping to see things from a different angle that might shed some new light on the case.

Finally, Jo said, "I think we need to add the Woodsons to our collection here."

Bridget nodded slowly. "But we're not sure they are involved."

"Still, they could be a piece of the puzzle. And who knows, maybe they know something." Jo reached into the bottom drawer and pulled out an old photo album. With a pang of sad nostalgia, Bridget recognized it as being the one her mom had in the bookshelf in the living room.

"We probably have some pictures of them in here, and we can put that on the door," Jo said. "Visuals are very powerful."

They perched on the edge of Jo's bed, the album creaking open to release echoes of their past, the photos a parade of outdated hairstyles and furniture from a life once whole.

There was Tammy, just a child and forever young on the glossy pages, wearing her favorite shirt—sunshine yellow with white daisies—now a grim reminder of the day she vanished. That was the very shirt she was wearing that day. Bridget's heart squeezed, the weight of old grief fresh as the image seared itself anew into her memory.

"Here's one from one of the summer cookouts," Jo

pointed out, flipping through the fragile memories. "Let's see... Ah, perfect for the armoire's door."

The photo they chose was a moment captured in time. Mrs. Woodson, maternal and smiling, with Tammy—a younger version, her tiny hand clutching Mrs. Woodson's shiny gold initial necklace—sitting on her lap. And there, the patriarchal figure of Mr. Woodson, a silent guardian.

"Remember how Tammy loved jewelry?" Bridget smiled at the memory. Their little sister had loved anything shiny and would grab out and clutch it in her tiny fist.

"Especially that crystal necklace Mom had, the one that reflected like a prism."

"Yeah, Tammy ripped it off her neck one time and it dropped onto the kitchen floor. Mom was so upset. But it only got a tiny chip."

"Mom never wore that again after Tammy was taken," Jo said somberly.

Gently, they slid the photograph from its sleeve and pinned it to the armoire's door—a new piece in the puzzle that was Tammy's disappearance. It joined the tapestry of clues, a silent hope that maybe this time, it would lead them to an answer long awaited.

CHAPTER FIFTEEN

Kevin straightened his uniform and took a deep breath as he nudged the door to the police station open. A sweet, sugary aroma wafted up from the bag of donuts in his grip. Had Bridget told Jo that she'd noticed Kevin was confused about where to file things?

He knew Bridget had noticed and if Sam and Jo found out how bad his memory really was, he was afraid they would make him go back out on leave. That was the last thing Kevin wanted. He wanted to get back to being out in the field. Sure, his memory was still a little shaky, but it wasn't that bad. Was it?

As he crossed the threshold, his gaze flicked around the reception area. Reese had almost finished painting, and the place looked good. She wasn't at the desk, though, so he continued past the old post office boxes into the squad room.

Lucy saw him before anyone else and rushed over, tail wagging and eyes bright. It warmed Kevin's heart that she was so happy to see him.

"Hey, girl, how ya doing?" He petted her with his free hand.

"Meow!" Major seemed to take offense to Lucy getting all the attention, so Kevin gave him a pat as well. Thankfully, the cat didn't scratch him—you never knew when Major would lash out.

Jo and Wyatt had been working at their desks. Jo's eyes lit up at the sight of the donut bag.

"Good morning," she exclaimed, a grin spreading across her face as she reached for the bag. Kevin had made sure to include a few of her favorite jelly donuts. Kevin's worry ebbed slightly, the corners of his mouth lifting in genuine relief. Jo wasn't looking at him differently, and he took that to mean that Bridget hadn't said anything.

They pulled chairs to the center of the room and passed the donut bag around, the ritual of morning coffee knitting the team closer together. Sam emerged from his office, and Kevin held his breath, but when Sam clapped him on the back and said that it was good to see things getting back to normal, Kevin knew he was in the clear.

The banter was casual, familiar, and then easily segued into the case. Jo hadn't made much progress, but Wyatt had collected April's things from the motel and was trying to get into her computer and dig around. Settling into the rhythm of the morning briefing, Kevin found his footing in the flow of information. "The gun... Why wipe it clean if it wasn't the murder weapon?" His brow furrowed in thought.

"Distraction, maybe, or just habit," Sam suggested, his eyes narrowing on a map pinned with various markers. "It did kill the owl. Maybe April's killer had the gun in his hand and then wiped it clean."

"But then why hit April with a log if he had the gun?" Wyatt asked.

Sam shrugged and bit into a chocolate glazed.

Kevin nodded, his thoughts already pacing ahead. "And the bandana, found by Lucy away from the crime scene in the woods. Could it be a marker of some sort?"

Wyatt leaned back in his chair, fingers drumming a silent rhythm on the desktop. "Or maybe even not related. You know how people party in those woods and drop all kinds of trash."

Sam nodded. "True, but not usually near the owl

sanctuary. The big party spot is on the other side of the forest."

The dialogue continued, the team tossing ideas back and forth until Kevin's voice cut through, carrying a thread of fresh perspective. "Why the owl sanctuary? The time of death puts them there in the middle of the night. Kind of a strange time to be there."

The room stilled, the significance of the location hanging between them like a clue begging to be deciphered.

Jo's expression grew contemplative, her mind visibly turning over the pieces. "That's a good point. But it's secluded, remote. A good place to kill someone and not be seen, if you know about it. You can get in and out through the construction site, and no one would notice."

"But it is also a place that is visited early in the morning, so the killer must have known that would happen," Sam added.

"Maybe it's personal?" Wyatt proposed. "Or symbolic?"

Kevin watched as Jo scribbled a note, her eyes alight with the thrill of the chase.

The discussion of the crime scene morphed into strategy, the team's collective focus narrowing. And there, in the midst of maps and markers, donuts, and coffee, Kevin's place on the team felt reaffirmed.

Sam stood and chugged down the rest of his coffee. "Jo and I are heading out to Mel's paint store. It's a long shot, but maybe he'll recall someone buying those specific colors splattered on the bandana."

Kevin felt a pang of envy. He willed himself to have patience. He'd get out in the field in due time.

Reese breezed into the room, the energy around her shifting like the sudden gust of a new weather front. She snagged a donut from the box with a grin. "Thanks for the breakfast, Kev."

The phone's shrill ring cut through the early morning calm. Reese moved to answer it, the informal dispatcher and multitasker of the precinct. "White Rock PD."

"Yes, Mrs. Holscher," Reese said into the phone, the hint of a smirk tugging at the corner of her mouth. "Your rose bush, you say?"

The room was silent except for the muffled voice on the other end of the line, punctuated by Reese's responses.

"I don't think we have a law against that, Mrs. Holscher," Reese continued, her smirk blooming into a restrained smile. The rest of them couldn't help but mirror the expression.

"Monetary damages? You'll have to talk to a lawyer for that," she added, scribbling something on a notepad. The pen paused momentarily. "Yes. Now calm down, Rita."

She glanced up at Sam and Jo, her eyes twinkling with the unspoken acknowledgment of the absurdity of the situation.

"I'll see if I can get someone to come out," she promised before hanging up.

Reese let out a chuckle. "Rita's on the war path. She says Nettie's chicken pecked up her rose bush. She wants someone to go out."

Sam shook his head, the barest hint of amusement in his gaze as he turned from Reese to the rest of the team. Jo's lips quirked in a knowing smirk, while Wyatt's fingers flew over his keyboard, the steady clatter a backdrop to the quieter drama.

Wyatt glanced up, his eyes squinting from the strain of screens and secrets. "I can swing by Rita's after this," he offered, though everyone knew his expertise was too vital to be spared for a neighborhood tiff.

"Nah, stick to cracking those passwords," Sam countered, his voice low and firm. "We need into April's digital life ASAP."

Sam turned to Kevin. Kevin's heartbeat picked up,

a mix of nerves and excitement making his hands feel unusually clammy.

"Do you feel ready to take on Rita?" Sam's question was casual, but it carried the weight of a test.

Kevin could barely nod before the keys to the Crown Vic spun through the air toward him. He snatched them from their arc, the jingle of authority loud in his grip. A smile split his face, broad and bright.

Sam's lips quirked. "Rita will appreciate the pomp. And we can always use the goodwill."

"I'm on it," Kevin replied, his voice steadier than he felt. The keys were warm, the metal edges biting slightly into his palm—a reminder of responsibility and the trust now placed in him.

The team returned to their tasks, but Kevin couldn't stop smiling as he moved to the door.

CHAPTER SIXTEEN

S am, Jo, and Lucy made their way to the paint store, nodding to townspeople and stopping for kids to pet Lucy. Some people greeted them warmly. Others avoided them. They were used to it.

"About time the police station got a touch-up, huh?" one of the locals commented with a grin. Either they had misinterpreted the purpose of their visit or knew about Reese's painting project.

Inside the paint store, the smell of turpentine and sawdust mingled in the air. The store was an organized chaos of color swatches and dusty paint cans. Behind the counter stood Mel, a gruff old man with a shock of white hair that matched the streaks on his apron. His hands were permanently stained with the testimony of his trade, and his eyes, though sharp, carried the gentle weariness of years of experience.

Sam and Jo approached the counter.

Mel scratched the stubble on his chin, a smudge of white paint highlighting a weathered crease on his cheek. "Ran out of paint, did ya?" He cocked a grizzled eyebrow at Sam. "Told that girl Reese she'd need another gallon, at least."

Sam shook his head. "No, not here for paint, Mel. We've got something else on our minds." He showed him a picture of the bandana on his phone. "See these paint splatters? You recall anyone buying paint like this?"

Mel peered at the fabric, his eyes squinting as if the colors might jump out with a clearer explanation. "Those garish colors? Nope. Can't say I do. Who'd want their walls to scream like a carnival midway?"

Sam's mouth twitched at the corners, almost a smile. "Well, we're thinking the person who chose them might not be aiming for *Homes and Gardens'* approval."

Mel let out a dry laugh, shaking his head. "Sorry, can't help ya. My customers have better taste than that."

Jo, who had been quiet, piped up. "Are you sure, Mel? It could be important."

The old man shrugged, a gesture that spoke of a long life of seeing too much yet never enough. "Maybe someone bought it at another store. There are plenty around. I think I'd remember those colors."

Sam put his phone in his pocket. "Thanks, Mel. If you think of anything, let us know."

Mel gave a noncommittal grunt, already turning back to his work, his mind on the paint and brushes that were his world.

Sam and Jo stepped out into the sunlight, the door jingling a goodbye behind them.

Sam nodded. "You win a few, you lose a few. Come on, let's get Lucy back in the Tahoe."

Sam closed the Tahoe's door, securing Lucy in the back. His eyes fixed on a figure across the street. A man in a tan-and-black baseball cap was slipping a pack of cigarettes into his coat pocket.

Jo followed Sam's gaze. "Didn't Jackson say he saw someone with a cap like that lurking around the sanctuary?"

"Yeah, he did." Sam's voice was flat, his gaze still locked on the man who looked like he was staring into some sort of art gallery. "And look who it is. Ricky Webster."

Jo's eyebrows drew together, a wrinkle forming on her forehead. "Ricky? That's weird."

Ricky had been a suspect in their last case and had been cleared, but Sam always thought there was something weird about him.

They watched Ricky light a cigarette, his movements furtive, a twitch in his shoulders as if he were expecting someone—or running from something.

"We should have a chat with him," Jo suggested, already stepping off the curb.

Sam nodded. "Let's not spook him."

They approached casually, with the practiced nonchalance of seasoned officers.

"Hey, Ricky," Sam said, not unkindly.

Ricky turned, a plume of smoke trailing from his lips. His eyes flicked over Sam and Jo, landing on Lucy with a hint of a smile before darting back to the officers. "Hey. What's the pleasure?"

"We were just admiring your cap," Jo said, tilting her head. "It's quite distinctive."

Ricky tapped a finger against the brim, his smile now fixed. "Got it at the conservation meet last month."

"Really?" Sam couldn't picture Ricky being a member of the conservation committee. "Because we've got a witness who saw a cap just like that near the owl sanctuary. Around the time April was killed."

Ricky's face tightened, the smoke curling between them like a barrier. "A lot of guys have caps like this."

"But not a lot of guys were seen wearing them near a crime scene," Jo pressed. Her voice was steady, but her eyes were sharp as flint.

Ricky's gaze flicked between them, calculating. "You think I got something to do with that mess? I heard it happened at the owl sanctuary, and I haven't been near there."

"We're just talking, Ricky," Sam assured him, his tone even. "But if there's anything you want to get off your chest..."

Ricky's fingers crushed the cigarette, dropping it to the ground and stamping it out. "I ain't got nothing to say. Not without a lawyer."

Hazel Webster, Ricky's grandmother, emerged from the bookstore they were standing in front of. Her hair was a crown of wiry gray, each strand rebelling against the notion of being tamed. The lines on her face told stories of a life chiseled by hardship, and her eyes—sharp as flint—had a reputation for setting any nosy officer straight.

She caught sight of Sam and Jo, and her lips pinched together. "What's this now?" she demanded, her voice like gravel stirred in a bucket. "You lot got nothing better to do than badger my grandson?"

Ricky stood a pace behind, his lips forming into a smirk as he watched his grandmother stand up to Sam and Jo.

Sam doffed his hat, a gesture of respect that did little to soften Hazel's scowl. "Ma'am, we assure you, we were just having a word with Ricky. Nothing to be concerned about."

Hazel snorted, a clear sign she wasn't buying a word. "A word, eh? Your 'words' have a way of turning into trouble. He's a good boy. Takes care of his grandma, don't you, Ricky?"

Ricky nodded, his cheeks tinged with a flush of embarrassment. "I was just helping Gran with the shopping," he said, his voice a quiet testament to his decency.

With a wary eye still fixed on the officers, Hazel handed Ricky her bag and looped her arm through his. As they began to walk away, Sam and Jo offered parting apologies, which Hazel dismissed with a harrumph that ricocheted off the store windows.

Once across the street, Sam spared a glance over his shoulder. Ricky was gently guiding Hazel, his attentiveness a stark contrast to the scene that had just unfolded.

Jo, watching alongside Sam, remarked quietly, "He does seem like the caring-grandson type."

Sam's lips pressed into a thin line, his eyes never leaving Ricky's retreating figure.

"Sometimes," he said, his voice dropping to a murmur meant for Jo alone, "the ones who seem the nicest have the most to hide."

CHAPTER SEVENTEEN

Sam and Jo pulled into the police station to find Marnie Wilson hammering a "Marnie for Mayor" sign into the precinct's front lawn. Today, she was dressed in an outfit that Jo always thought of as her *common man* outfit. Jeans and a flannel shirt—something a blue-collar worker would wear.

Marnie's eyes lifted, catching sight of Sam, and for a fleeting moment, they softened, betraying a warmth reserved just for him.

"Marnie." Sam's voice held a professional detachment, a barricade against any personal undertones. "The lawn of a police station might not be the ideal place for campaign material."

"Oh, come on, Sam," she coaxed, a playful tilt in her words. "It's public property."

Jo, standing a step behind, watched the exchange, her lips pressed into a thin line. She didn't trust the gleam in Marnie's eye nor the coy dance of politics. Lucy, ever the barometer of intent, sniffed disinterestedly at Marnie before trotting back to Jo's side, aligning herself with the silent sentiment.

Sam didn't bite, his indifference to Marnie's charms as solid as the badge on his chest. "Just doesn't seem right," he said. "Might look like the department is picking sides."

Her smile flickered, but she recovered quickly, gesturing toward the ruckus down the street. "Looks like Jamison has bigger fish to fry," she said.

The crowd outside the mayor's office was a mess of noise and anger. Signs jabbed the air—Owl Killer, Fairness to the Birds. They were a loud bunch, getting louder as Jo and Sam approached.

Jo's gaze fixed on the nearest sign, the words a blunt accusation. Owl Killer. The message was clear, the crowd's mood uglier by the second. She could feel the tension in the air, thick enough to choke on.

Sam caught her eye, and without a word, they edged closer to the action. The protesters didn't let up, their shouts bouncing off the buildings, calling for justice, for answers.

The cacophony from the Owl Protection Society cut through the morning air, their outrage over the unsolved owl murder palpable. Flustered, Mayor Jamison tugged Sam to the side, his voice laced with desperation. "Can't you clear them out?"

"They're exercising their rights, as long as they keep it peaceful," Sam countered, his gaze fixed on the protestors. Jamison's eyes darted to the police station, narrowing at the sight of Marnie Wilson. "Is that Marnie putting up her campaign sign?" he grumbled.

"Yeah, that's her. I've tried to talk her out of it," Sam replied, watching Marnie give her sign one final push into the soft earth.

Jamison's face twisted with suspicion. "She could be orchestrating this spectacle," he muttered.

Sam exchanged a skeptical look with Jo. While he doubted Marnie's involvement, the dirty tricks of political games were not lost on him. Every move was calculated, and if Marnie had indeed played her hand in this, it was a shrewd one. Sam's mind turned over the possibilities as he surveyed the scene, and he wondered how far Marnie would actually go to win the race.

If she was involved in the Owl Protection Society's presence here, was she just taking advantage of the death of the owl, or did she have something to do with it? Sam doubted she would go that far.

A tall man stepped up to the group. He stood out in stark contrast with the casual attire of the townspeople. His suit was impeccably tailored, and his polished demeanor spoke of boardrooms rather than back roads. His hair, dark and perfectly coifed, caught the afternoon light, and his eyes—just as dark—swept over the scene with an unreadable expression.

"Good afternoon, Mayor," he greeted with a nod that was both respectful and slightly aloof.

Jamison's response was a narrowed gaze, tinged with recognition. "Victor, what brings you here?" he asked, his tone a mix of surprise and caution.

Jamison turned his attention to Sam. "Do you know Victor Sorentino?" he inquired with an undertone that suggested a complicated history.

Sam, who had been sizing up the newcomer with a lawman's critical eye, extended his hand. "Can't say that I do. Sam Mason, chief of police." He introduced himself then gestured to his right. "This is Sergeant Jody Harris."

The handshake between Sam and Victor was firm, each man gauging the other. Victor's smile was polished, yet it didn't quite reach his eyes, which remained cool and detached. "A pleasure. I'm the senior public liaison for Convale," he stated, his voice carrying an edge of authority.

The man's refined exterior, coupled with the underlying hardness in his demeanor, suggested a narrative far richer than his title implied. Sam couldn't shake the feeling that behind Victor Sorentino's cultivated smile lay a realm of unsaid words and veiled intentions.

"So, what does a senior public liaison do, exactly?" Jo asked.

Sam watched Victor carefully, a silent bet with himself that the title was corporate speak for someone tasked with making sure Convale's image stayed spotless.

Victor's smile never wavered as he answered Jo. "My role is to inform the public about our initiatives. I let them know what's on the horizon, how we're advancing our energy programs and ensuring they receive the best service at the lowest cost," he explained, each word sounding practiced and polished.

Mayor Jamison, clearly still uneasy, probed further. "Why are you here, Victor? Are you part of the Owl Protection Society?"

"No," Victor replied smoothly. "I just make it a

point to stay abreast of the town's significant events." His eyes held Jamison's, a gleam surfacing as he added, "Though it doesn't seem to cast you in the best light, what with the election coming up."

With that, Victor acknowledged Jo and Sam with a nod. "Pleasure to meet both of you," he said before turning on his heel and walking off with a grace that felt out of place in the midst of the protest.

Sam's frown deepened as he watched Victor walk away, the man's presence leaving an uneasy echo. "Odd guy," he muttered, more to himself than anyone else.

Jo nodded, her arms crossed as she watched Victor's retreating figure. "Yeah, I get a weird vibe from him," she said, her voice tinged with suspicion.

Mayor Jamison, who had been silent, unfolded his arms and let out a huff. "He's always looming where he's not wanted," he grumbled, eyeing the spot where Victor had stood just moments ago.

Sam's gaze swept over the crowd. "They seem peaceful so far," he remarked, his voice laced with the tension of the afternoon. "If things get out of hand, give me a call." He didn't like the uncertainty of the situation, the potential for a spark to ignite chaos.

As Sam and Jo turned to leave, Sam's mind was already churning, his thoughts returning to their main priority. "We need to stay focused on the bigger problem—finding out who killed April," he said firmly, the weight of responsibility pressing down on him.

Jo glanced back at the crowd then at the outline of the sanctuary in the distance. "And the owl."

CHAPTER EIGHTEEN

Jo's scowl was almost audible as they passed the "Marnie for Mayor" sign in front of the police station. "That's kind of close to the curb. Hope no one runs it over," she said, the corner of her mouth twitching in amusement.

The squad room was a welcome respite. Jo went straight to the K-Cup coffee maker, her movements fluid and practiced.

Jo glanced over her shoulder, her hand hovering over the assortment of K-Cups. "Coffee, Sam?" Without waiting for his response—she knew it would be a yes—she called out across the room, "Wyatt, you want one?"

From his desk cluttered with papers and tech equipment, Wyatt barely looked up, his eyes glued to

April's computer screen as he worked to crack the passwords. "Sure," he mumbled, absorbed in his task.

The soft hum of the machine filled the space as Jo selected the pods, dropping one into the holder for Sam. Sam watched the dark liquid dribble into his navy blue WRPD mug, his thoughts momentarily adrift to the protestors outside.

"Hope that owl protest dies down soon," he mused aloud, leaning against the counter.

Jo smirked, pressing her own mug—a vintage seventies yellow smiley mug she'd found at a yard sale —against the dispenser. "Kinda fun to see Jamison sweat, though." Her eyes sparkled with mischief.

Lucy patrolled the room, her nose skimming the floor tiles. Every so often, she'd pause, sniffing more intently, before moving on to the next potential clue in her canine investigation. She paid particular attention to the corners and under the desks.

Jo picked up the extra mug of coffee, the steam curling up in soft tendrils, and walked over to Wyatt's desk. She placed it next to his mouse pad, nudging it into his line of sight. "Here," she said.

Wyatt, his fingers never ceasing their dance across the keyboard, grunted a distracted, "Thanks," his eyes not leaving the screen.

Coffee delivered, Jo turned and strolled back to her own space, her steps slowing as she neared Lucy. She reached down to give the German shepherd a gentle pat on the head. "What are you hunting for, huh?" she asked playfully. Lucy's response was a nudge against Jo's hand and a brief glance before resuming her sniff patrol.

Jo's gaze drifted to the empty spot atop the filing cabinet where Major usually perched. "Looking for Major? If so, be careful what you wish for." Major was probably tucked away in a closet guarding his latest toy, and Jo could only imagine the chaos that would happen if Lucy poked her nose in there.

"How are things going?" Sam asked Wyatt. "Was there anything on her phone? Her belongings?"

Wyatt's chair groaned as he leaned back, his eyes finally detaching from the glow of the computer screen to meet Sam's expectant look. He passed a hand through his longish hair, pulling at the ends in a gesture of fatigue.

"She only had some clothes and a duffle bag. Her phone was in her pocket, so I worked with John on that." Wyatt squinted as his eyes adjusted to the broader light of the room.

"Find anything?" Sam asked.

Wyatt shook his head. "Just a few texts, but they're

very basic. One was to Travis and another to Archie Wells, confirming appointments."

"Nothing personal? No calls?" Sam furrowed his brow.

"Not a single one." Wyatt took a gulp of his coffee. "If she had another phone, it wasn't in her motel room."

"And the computer?" Sam nodded toward the open laptop.

"Not much to go on," he admitted. "Cracked her password, though."

Sam leaned against the edge of Wyatt's desk, arms folded, a silent prompt for more information.

"The bank account's the only thing sticking out," Wyatt continued, taking another sip of coffee.

"Interesting how?" Sam prodded, his voice low, matching the hum of concentration that filled the squad room.

Wyatt set the mug down, a slight clink against the wood. "Her account's seen some peculiar activity. Large sums. Cash deposits."

"That seems to support what Archie said about her extorting money," Jo said from her desk.

"Sure does," Sam agreed.

"And only one check written." Wyatt looked back at his screen. "To the motel."

Sam's brows rose. "At least that's a lead."

"And something else." Wyatt nudged a small pocket calendar across his desk toward Sam. "There are a few notes in there about meetings, all with initials, but one very interesting note on the day she died."

Sam leaned forward to look at the calendar. It was inside a plastic bag and lay open to the current week. The entry on the day April died had simply the initials H.M. and the time ten p.m.

"Any idea who H.M. is?" Sam asked.

Wyatt shook his head. "I'm searching through her computer now."

Sam stood. "Good job. Looks like we might have a few more leads to follow."

"Finally, we are starting to get somewhere." Jo sipped her coffee and looked at the empty desk. "Have you heard from Kevin? I hope Nettie and Rita aren't giving him a hard time."

CHAPTER NINETEEN

"Officer Kevin, look at this! That ornery chicken has devoured my prize-winning rose bush!" Rita demanded, her hands planted firmly on her hips.

Kevin looked down at the rose bush. It was too late in the season for blooming, but he could see quite a few peck holes at the base.

Nettie retorted with equal vigor, "And that goat of hers ate my new housecoat. It was drying on the line, and now it's ruined!"

The two women, both widows well into their seventies, stood on the border of their adjoining properties, their arms crossed over their chests, their brows knitted in both annoyance and a faint plea for attention.

Kevin stood between them, the unlikely arbitrator. "Now, ladies," he began, the corners of his mouth struggling against the urge to smile. "We can't have this feud every other week."

Rita's sharp eyes softened a bit. "Well, I wouldn't say a thing if her feathered beast didn't terrorize my garden."

"And I'd keep quiet if her goat didn't have a taste for laundry!" Nettie shot back.

Kevin nodded, understanding the undercurrent of loneliness that often prompted their disputes. "Rita, I'm going to bring you a new rose bush this weekend. How does that sound?"

Nettie's eyebrows rose. "Since when is gardening a service of the police department?"

Kevin straightened up, all business now. "It is now," he said, and the simple statement seemed to settle the matter.

Rita beamed, the creases in her face deepening with genuine joy. "Well then, Officer Kevin, I'll have to make you my famous fruitcake as a thank-you. Not that dried-up old thing Nettie makes."

Nettie huffed, but the sparkle in her eye gave away her affection for her old friend. "My fruitcake isn't dry. It's traditional."

They both looked to Kevin, expecting him to take

sides, but he just shook his head, the image of peace-keeping authority. "Now, now, no need for any more of that. We're all neighbors here."

There was a beat of silence before Rita offered a truce. "I'll trim back Bitsy's roaming area. No more housecoat incidents, Nettie."

"And I'll... I'll keep the chicken on my side," Nettie conceded but only with a playful roll of her eyes.

Kevin tipped his hat. "Thank you, ladies. You both make White Rock the place I'm proud to serve."

He climbed back into the cruiser, a feeling of accomplishment blooming in his chest. He'd done it! His first call since being out of the hospital, and it had gone as smooth as butter.

As he looked in the rearview mirror, Nettie and Rita were already chatting over the fence, their argument forgotten as quickly as it had ignited.

As calls went, this one was pretty run-of-the-mill. Maybe that was a good thing since he didn't have his service gun back yet. But it was a big step forward. So far, he'd been relegated to office work and organizing things in the evidence room that they shared with other regional police departments. In fact, he was scheduled to work the evidence room that afternoon.

He chose the scenic route back to town, allowing the thread of roads less traveled to draw him away from the straight path home. The old diner appeared almost as an afterthought along the road that was once more highly traveled, a drab structure that stubbornly defied the passage of time.

Kevin had eaten in the diner a few times. The food wasn't that great. He supposed it had once been better back when this was the main road and the diner got more traffic. Right now, only three cars were parked outside, and it looked fairly empty inside.

The woman sitting at the booth by the window caught his attention. There was something familiar about her. Wait... Wasn't that Jo's sister?

Kevin slowed the car. Bridget's presence there was unmistakably out of place, her innocent air clashing with the seedy atmosphere of the diner.

The man she was with raised a red flag in Kevin's seasoned mind. His demeanor, even viewed from a distance, screamed trouble. Was Bridget in some kind of trouble? She'd kept his secret about the filing cabinet, and he wanted to return the favor by helping her... if she needed it.

Kevin pulled into the parking lot. At the least, he could use a cup of coffee. If she was fine, he would leave reassured. If not, he'd be there to assist.

BRIDGET STIRRED HER COFFEE ABSENTMINDEDLY, the spoon clinking against the mug in a slow, rhythmic pattern. The diner, once a beacon along the highway, now looked like a relic from a bygone era. Its walls looked greasy and dirty. The stainless-steel counter must have once gleamed with fresh paint but was now dulled and sapped of vibrancy. Fluorescent lights buzzed overhead, casting an unflattering glow over the handful of patrons scattered across peeling vinyl booths.

When Bridget lived on the streets, having a meal in a diner like this would have seemed like heaven. She'd adjusted to her new life already. But there was one good thing about the diner—Jo wouldn't see her in here. Not that she was hiding, but the fewer reasons Jo had to worry, the better.

Even though Bridget hadn't seen anyone following her, she'd figured that it was better to be safe than sorry, so she'd reached out to Carl Denozi, one of her friends from her past life, to see if he knew anything. It wouldn't be a bad idea to keep in touch in case she ever needed his vast array of not-so-legal services.

Her sandwich lay half-eaten, the bread slightly stale. Carl's burger was a mess of grease and condiments, but he seemed to like it. They spoke of old times, of people who had been mere whispers on the street. Some names brought a faint smile to Bridget's lips, others a shadow of concern.

Carl took a deliberate bite of his burger, the juiciness of the patty seeping into the bun as he chewed thoughtfully. Bridget sipped her coffee, watching the steam curl upward before dissipating into the stale air of the diner.

"You heard anything about Annie?" Bridget asked. Annie had been a sweet girl, way too young for a life on the streets.

Carl wiped his mouth with the back of his hand, shaking his head. "Annie's just... vanished, you know?" He sighed. "It's a rough life out there. Not everyone's cut out for the long haul."

Bridget's gaze dropped. "And Sheila?" she inquired, the name tasting bittersweet on her lips.

"Heard she's trying to patch things up with her folks," Carl replied, a hint of respect in his tone. "Went back home to clear her head. Maybe she'll make it out."

She nodded, a small smile flickering. "Good for her," Bridget murmured. "Everyone deserves a shot at a second act."

They fell into a contemplative quiet, mulling over the fragility of the paths they'd each taken. The silence was comfortable, filled with shared understanding and the ghosts of friends who'd slipped through the cracks.

Carl took a swig of his drink, peering over the rim of his cup at her. "Why bring them up, Bridget? You thinking of heading back... to that life?"

Bridget shook her head quickly, her fingers tight around her mug. "No, it's not that. It's just... knowing where people end up, it helps. Keeps you grounded, you know?"

Bridget studied Carl. He was different now, more cautious. But Bridget wondered if beneath that veneer of change, the old connections lingered.

"Are you still... you know, connected?" she ventured, her voice low.

Surprise flickered across Carl's face. He leaned back, appraising her with a new level of scrutiny. "You looking for a piece of the action?" he asked, the question hanging in the air like smoke.

"Not like that," Bridget rushed to clarify. "It's just... up here, in the woods, a girl's gotta fend for herself."

Carl's eyes narrowed into slits, the easygoing façade slipping. "Into something, Bridget?" he prodded. There was a hardness in his voice, a hint of the street sharpness that could cut through lies.

She shook her head, her fingers wrapped tightly around her coffee mug. "Nothing like that," she repeated. "Just... making sure I can protect myself if the past comes back to haunt me."

A silence settled between them, loaded and tense. Carl's gaze didn't waver, as if he was trying to decipher a hidden message in her words. Bridget held his stare, her own resolve steeling.

Finally Carl nodded. "Yeah, I'm connected. What do you need?"

"Nothing too big. Just something small. Personal protection." Life on the street had taught Bridget a few things, and one of those was how to handle guns. She wouldn't be able to get one through legal channels so didn't have much of a choice. She didn't need anything big, didn't want anything conspicuous. Hopefully, she'd never have to use it anyway.

"Okay. It might take a while, but I'll see what I can find for you."

The bell over the diner's door jingled, cutting through the static atmosphere. Bridget looked up, momentarily startled by a police uniform. Not Jo, thankfully. It was Kevin.

Kevin ambled to the counter. "Coffee, please," Kevin said, nodding toward the pot with a faint smile.

As Doris poured the dark brew into a thick, white mug, Kevin's eyes wandered over to Bridget. Their gazes met, and she lifted her hand in a small wave.

"Hey there," Kevin greeted, walking over to her booth. "Didn't expect to see you here."

A hint of suspicion colored his tone as his eyes flicked to Carl. Carl was already on his feet, tossing a twenty-dollar bill on the table.

"Nice to catch up with you, Bridget," Carl said, a hint of haste in his voice. "Gotta run." With a nod that didn't quite seem directed at either Bridget or Kevin, he brushed past Kevin and out the door.

As Carl's presence faded, Bridget gestured to the now-vacant seat across from her.

"Take a seat, Kevin," she offered, her eyes following Carl's retreat through the window.

Kevin slid into the booth, placing his coffee on the table.

"You okay?" he asked, a tinge of concern threading his voice.

"Yeah, just an old friend," Bridget replied, though her eyes stayed on the door a moment longer before finally meeting Kevin's. "What brings you out this way? Don't tell me my sister has you spying on me."

He shook his head, the amusement clear in his eyes. "Hardly," he replied. "I was out on a call and just driving by. Needed a coffee." He lifted his mug, as if the coffee were evidence enough of his innocent intentions.

Then his expression softened, his eyes holding a quiet empathy. "Why would Jo need to spy on you?" he asked softly, genuinely curious.

Bridget's cheeks tinged with color, and she looked away briefly before meeting his gaze again. "Jo's just... overprotective. Since I was an addict and lived on the streets," she confessed. "I've worked hard to clean up my act, and I think she's worried I might fall back."

Straightening up in the booth, Bridget's voice carried a firm resolve. "I have no intention of going back, but Carl... Well, he's from that old life. Sometimes it's good to keep in touch."

Kevin nodded as if understanding the complex pull of past connections.

Her gaze dropped momentarily then lifted to peek up at him from under her lashes—a mix of vulnerability and trust in her eyes. "You won't tell Jo, will you?" she asked.

Kevin's response was immediate, his voice quiet but firm. "Your secret's safe with me," he assured her. "We all have secrets. And I know you noticed I couldn't remember where to file things. You didn't tell Jo, so I guess we're even. We'll keep each other's secrets."

Bridget considered his words, a hint of playfulness appearing in her eyes. "Sort of like a pact?"

Kevin laughed, a short, hearty sound. "Sort of," he agreed.

Extending her hand across the table, Bridget offered a tangible sign of their mutual understanding. "Then I guess we should shake on it."

Kevin placed his hand in hers, and for a moment, they both acknowledged the gravity of their shared confidences with a firm handshake. As they did, Bridget couldn't help but notice the strength and warmth in his grasp, and it felt reassuring—a silent affirmation of their newly formed bond.

CHAPTER TWENTY

In the squad room, Jo stared at her screen, the cursor blinking back at her with a kind of indifferent challenge. She'd hit a wall with April Summers. The digital world was keeping its secrets close this time.

The research into people with the initials H.M. hadn't been much more successful. She hadn't struck out, but there were hundreds of them.

"Any luck?" Sam asked, glancing over from his desk piled with his own leads to nowhere.

Jo rubbed her temples. "I'm swimming in a sea of H.M.s. Six hundred and counting. It's like looking for a needle in a haystack... if the haystack were made of needles."

Sam let out a dry chuckle. "That's one prickly haystack."

The sound of the front door opening announced Reese's entrance. After a few minutes of rustling sounds, Reese appeared at the doorway of the squad room, all bubbly and smiles.

Jo caught a twinkle in Reese's eyes. "What's up? It looks like you are bursting to tell us something."

Reese's grin widened, lighting up her face. "Oh, it's nothing to do with our cases. I've brought a piece of artwork for the reception area. I'd love to hear what you all think," she said, her gaze eagerly shifting from Jo to Sam and then to Wyatt. Her excitement was palpable, like that of a child showing off a new toy.

Led by their curiosity, the trio followed Reese out of the squad room. As they approached the reception area, Reese held the artwork with a flourish reminiscent of a game show host revealing a grand prize. The painting, however, was a stark contrast to her enthusiasm.

Jo scrutinized the canvas, her brows knitting in confusion. It was a chaotic ensemble of colors and shapes. Bold splotches of paint, ranging from bright oranges to deep blues, clashed violently against each other. Startling greens swirled unpredictably, their edges blurred and undefined. Here and there, aggressive splatters of red seemed to burst from the canvas, like drops of blood in midexplosion. Amidst the chaos, streaks of yellow melted into their surroundings, giving off an impression of a solar flare caught in a cosmic dance.

Wyatt, usually not one to mince words, leaned closer to the artwork, squinting as if trying to decipher a hidden message among the vibrant chaos. The painting, in its abstract boldness, seemed to demand attention, yet its meaning, if there was any, remained elusive.

Sam, standing beside Jo, tilted his head slightly, his expression morphing into a puzzled frown. "What's it supposed to be?" he asked, his tone a mixture of bewilderment and curiosity.

"It's not 'supposed to be' anything. It's modern art," Reese replied, her enthusiasm slightly dampened by their puzzled reactions.

Wyatt, who had been studying the canvas with a critical eye, joined the conversation. "I don't know about modern art, but something tranquil might be more fitting. You know, a river or mountains... Something calming."

"Or a moose," Sam added with a half smile,

picturing a giant moose adorning their police station
wall.

They all turned expectantly toward Jo, who had
been observing the painting in silence. She was about
to comment when something about the chaos of colors
tugged at her detective instincts. The paint splotches,
the hues, and the shades... They were strangely familiar. A sudden realization struck her, and without a
word, she darted into Sam's office.

Returning moments later with the photograph of
the bandana in hand, she held it up next to the painting. The colors of the paint splatters on the canvas
were an uncanny match to those on the bandana. The
vibrant oranges, deep blues, startling greens—it was all
there.

"Reese, where exactly did you get this?" Jo asked,
her tone laced with a blend of urgency and excitement.

Reese, taken aback by Jo's sudden interest,
answered, "Oh, it's from a local artist. Her studio is
right next to the bookstore downtown. Lily Dunn is
her name."

Sam grabbed his keys from the hook on the wall.
"Looks like we're going shopping for a painting."

DUNN ART WAS an inviting palette of pastel hues, with a cornflower-blue awning trimmed in sunny yellow that fluttered gently in the soft breeze. Gorgeous paintings sat in the window, everything from serene landscapes to bold abstracts.

Warm light spilled from the interior onto the sidewalk, casting a welcoming glow that stood in stark contrast to the dimming sky. Inside, a young woman with an edgy pixie cut and a smock splattered with a spectrum of paint stains manned the register.

Her expression was one of easygoing welcome until her eyes registered their badges and uniforms. Her welcoming smile hesitated, the corners of her lips dipping slightly, as a shadow of concern crossed her features.

But then her gaze fell upon Lucy, and the woman's face visibly relaxed, a softness creeping back into her eyes as she regarded the dog, a universal icebreaker. Lucy always had the effect of setting people at ease.

Lucy sniffed at Lily's feet then looked up at Sam. A sure sign that Lucy recognized her scent, most likely from the bandana she'd found.

"Welcome to Dunn Art," she said, regaining her composure. "Can I help you find something?" Her attempt to sound casual was betrayed by the slight quaver in her voice, a clear sign she was uncertain about the nature of their visit.

"Are you Lily Dunn?" Sam asked.

"Yes, I'm Lily," she started tentatively, her initial professional tone faltering as her brain made the connection. Then, as realization dawned, her eyes widened slightly. "Oh, the painting for Reese! It's quite the statement piece, isn't it?" She forced a chuckle, her attempt at levity a thin veneer over her growing apprehension. "I'm thrilled it's in the station. I think."

Sam's lips twitched into a half smile, recognizing the defensive pride of an artist concerned for her work's reception. "It's definitely... distinctive," he said diplomatically. "But we're here about something else."

He held out the photo of the bandana, watching her closely. Her hand shot up to her throat, to the white bandana she wore, now smudged with splashes of various colors of paint. She twisted it beneath her fingers, a brief flash of a gold chain glinting underneath.

Sam studied Lily's face as he presented the picture of the bandana. "Does this look familiar?" he asked, his tone casual but his eyes intent.

Lily gave a noncommittal shrug. "Bandanas? Yeah, they're part of my look. It comes in handy to have one on if I need to wipe off some paint that I splattered," she said, trying to appear unfazed. "Lots of people wear them, though."

"But this one has paint on it," Sam pointed out, "similar to the colors in the artwork Reese bought from you."

Lily's eyes flickered between Sam and Jo, a hint of tension creeping into her demeanor. "Well, I guess it does. It could be mine," she said with forced lightness. "But what exactly are you getting at?"

Sam leaned in slightly. "Just wondering if it's yours. And if you might've been near the owl sanctuary recently?"

There was a flicker, a tiny spasm around her left eye, as she replied a bit too quickly, "Nope, haven't been around there."

The room hung heavy with silence as Sam held her gaze. Finally, Lily offered, "I do hike in the woods sometimes, though. Maybe I dropped it on a hike, and it somehow ended up over there? The wind blew it or an animal dragged it?"

Sam gave a slow, thoughtful nod. "Maybe," he conceded. "Well, if you weren't at the owl sanctuary, then that's all we need to know."

He turned to leave, with Jo following behind. At the door, Jo paused, glancing back at the colorful canvases that adorned the walls. "By the way, you do great work." Jo gestured broadly at her paintings.

The faintest smile washed over Lily's face as they departed, but her hand subconsciously twisted the bandana as she watched them leave.

Sam and Jo, with Lucy in tow, made their way back to the Tahoe parked along Main Street.

"So, what'd you think of that?" Sam inquired as they reached the SUV.

Jo glanced back at the shop, where Lily could still be seen through the front window, shuffling paintings on a wall, her motions betraying a hint of agitation. "She's hiding something, Sam. Did you see her? She was way too nervous."

Sam gave a thoughtful nod, his gaze lingering on the figure of Lily inside. "Lucy recognized her scent, but Lily did have a point about the possibility that she dropped the bandana elsewhere. But I agree, she is hiding something. You think she could have been up at the owl sanctuary?"

Jo opened the back door of the Tahoe, allowing Lucy to jump in before she climbed into the passenger seat. "Maybe," she mused, clicking her seat belt in place. "But did you notice her feet? Tiny. There's no way she could have made those prints we found. She can't be our killer if the killer is the one who left those tracks."

As Sam started the engine, his eyes met Jo's. "True, her feet don't match. But even if she isn't the killer," he said, his voice dropping to a lower, more contemplative tone, "she might have seen something or someone. And if she did, that makes her either a witness, an accomplice... or the next potential target."

CHAPTER TWENTY-ONE

Kevin stood amid the meticulous array of the regional evidence room, a space shared by the White Rock Police and neighboring districts, including the small, often-overlooked Berlin precinct. It was a quiet room, surrounded by the silent testimony of a hundred cases. He was cataloging a set of gold chains, the camera in his hand clicking with each snapshot he took for the database.

His brows drew together, concentration etched deep into his features as he worked. The chains glinted under the fluorescent lights, each number he entered a promise of order, a bulwark against the chaos that memory issues tried to bring into his life.

Kevin worked methodically, a process that had

become a grounding routine in the wake of his memory loss. His gloved hands moved with practiced ease, cataloging a series of items from an old narcotics case, each tagged and bagged, their relevance in court now expired.

He picked up a notepad from the pile, an afterthought among the more high-tech evidence. It was filled with scribbles of what looked like a programmer's shorthand—strings of characters, symbols, and numbers, a cryptographer's sketchbook. As he flipped through the pages, Kevin felt a pull in his mind, the sensation of a curtain fluttering in a long-abandoned room. A memory bubbled up. The thumb drive.

Without really knowing why, he pulled out his phone and began snapping pictures of each page, ensuring the focus was sharp, the detail clear. He paused over a particular string of alphanumeric characters that sparked a deep-seated recognition, a sequence that whispered to him of something important and personal.

With the notepad photographed, he emailed the pictures to his private account, a pang of urgency in his chest. He didn't have the thumb drive here—it was at home, tucked away in a drawer, its contents just out of mental reach—but he had a hunch. A hunch that the key to its secrets was contained within the scribbles of this notepad.

The door clicked open and Officer Daniels from Berlin stepped in, a friendly grin on his face that seemed so at odds with the solemnity of the room.

"Hey, Kevin. Need to pick up the B and E evidence from last week. Roberts needs it for a lineup."

"Should be in the back," Kevin replied, his voice steady, his gaze never leaving the screen. "I'll grab it for you in a sec."

Once the last serial number was entered and double-checked, Kevin pushed back his chair and stood, his back releasing a slight twinge of discomfort. He walked toward the back, his eyes scanning the meticulously organized shelves, but a seed of doubt crept into his mind.

He paused, his hand hovering over the shelf where the evidence was supposed to be. The quiet confidence that had carried him into the room began to crumble as his mind grasped at the memory of where he had placed it.

"Everything okay?" Officer Daniels called out, leaning casually against the door frame.

"Yeah, just give me a moment," Kevin replied, the words almost catching in his throat.

He pulled out his notebook, the one companion that never failed him, and flicked through the pages filled with his tidy, precise handwriting. His finger landed on the entry from last week, and relief washed over him.

"Moved Item #2047 for drug seizure items," he read aloud to himself, the tension in his shoulders easing.

Navigating to a different section with a resolve that belied his earlier confusion, Kevin located the item and handed it to Daniels.

"Thanks, Kevin. You're a lifesaver," the officer said with genuine gratitude, clasping the evidence bag.

As Daniels disappeared through the doorway, Kevin let out a breath of relief. The room felt larger suddenly, the shelves not just a storage space but a landscape he had to navigate with painstaking attention.

Returning to his computer, he entered the new location for the item, ensuring the digital record matched the physical one. Then, with methodical care, he scribbled down a reminder in his notebook.

His hands might have betrayed the subtlest of shakes, a silent herald of his internal struggle, but his spirit was steadfast. He pressed on, cataloging the next set of items, each entry a small victory in his quiet battle against forgetfulness. Thankfully, he only had another hour to go before he was off the clock. His brain needed a rest, but before that he had to see if anything he found in the notebook cracked the password on the thumb drive.

CHAPTER TWENTY-TWO

I n the cozy warmth of Jo's kitchen, the woods outside her window faded into the soft glow of twilight as Jo watched Bridget preparing food.

"Good thing you made a giant batch of this stuff," Jo quipped, unable to resist the alluring aroma. She deftly dipped a fork into the pot, aiming for a taste.

Bridget was quick to bat her hand away with a playful swat. "Why is that?" she inquired with a mock sternness that only siblings could share.

"Because Sam just called. Mick's got some lead on the case, and they're both heading over. Thought they might want to dig in," Jo explained, retracting her fork but not her interest in the meal.

Bridget's eyes lit up at the mention of additional

guests. "Really? That's great! More people to impress with my culinary skills." A smug smile played on her lips as she stirred the risotto, which was flecked with strands of orange.

"What's that orange stuff?" Jo leaned in closer, her voice dropping to a conspiratorial whisper as if discussing state secrets rather than dinner plans.

"Saffron," Bridget declared with a flourish, giving the creamy dish a final, confident stir.

Earlier, when Jo had walked through the door, the house was alive with homely smells, the gentle buzz of family life in the air. Pickles lounged on the porch, watching her warily from the corner as she approached but not running away. Finn was his usual bubbly self.

"I'll call Holden and see if he wants in. If we're discussing their case, he'll want to be here." Bridget reached for her phone. She dialed Holden with practiced ease, her excitement barely contained. Jo leaned against the counter, munching on a homemade buttermilk biscuit as she eavesdropped on the one-sided conversation.

"Hey, Holden, it's Bridget. Mick has some news on the case," she said.

There was a pause, a soft murmur from the phone that Jo couldn't quite catch.

"Yes, and I'm making supper too. Saffron risotto. So why don't you come over and bring your appetite with you?" Bridget continued, her invitation wrapped in the promise of a good meal and good company.

Another pause, this one longer, as Holden responded.

Bridget's laughter filled the kitchen, genuine and infectious. "No, I promise, nothing too fancy this time. You'll love it. See you soon?"

As Bridget ended the call, she looked over at Jo, her expression a mix of pride and anticipation. "Holden's on his way. Says he wouldn't miss home cooking for the world."

Sam arrived first with Lucy trotting at his heels, her tail wagging in anticipation of the household's welcome.

"Smells like heaven in here," he announced.

Jo looked up from where she was chopping fresh herbs. "Heaven's got nothing on Bridget's cooking," she teased, sliding the herbs into the risotto pot as Bridget had instructed her.

Lucy, ever the social butterfly, made her rounds, nudging and sniffing hellos, securing her place among friends.

A knock on the kitchen door surprised them. No

one ever used that door because it was around back and in the dark. Jo opened it cautiously to find Mick.

"Did you just come out of the woods or something?" Jo stood back to let him in.

Mick laughed. "Or something. Just checking around the place. You know how it is. Saw you all in here and figured I'd come in this way." Mick shrugged off his leather jacket and headed toward the liquor cabinet. "I hope you have whiskey."

Bridget glanced over her shoulder and chuckled. "Of course, we got the best for you."

Mick raised an eyebrow and made himself at home getting a small glass from the cupboard. "Anyone else?" he asked over the clink of ice and the slosh of liquid.

"I'll stick with beer," Sam said.

"Me too," Jo added.

Holden was the last to arrive, knocking and then pushing the door open with a soft creak. He had a bakery box in his hand. "Didn't want to come empty-handed."

Sam looked into the box. "Boston cream pie. My favorite."

Bridget plated the meal, and they all moved to the table, the chairs scraping softly against the floorboards as they sat down.

Holden, his gaze roving appreciatively over the spread, was the first to sink his fork into the risotto. "Oh, this is heavenly," he declared, his voice muffled by a mouthful of the creamy grains. The risotto was rich and complex, the saffron lending a luxurious earthiness.

Bridget watched the table with a mixture of pride and anticipation, her cheeks flushed from the heat of the stove and the warm glow of the overhead lights.

Sam savored a bite of the chicken. "The chicken's perfect. It always comes out too dry when I make it."

Mick spooned up some of the golden caramelized Brussels sprouts. "I only know how to grill, so my chicken comes out burned."

Jo leaned back in her chair, a forkful of risotto paused at her lips. "I hope Bridget never gets her own place. I've been eating like royalty since she came."

Laughter bubbled around the table, harmonizing with the clatter of cutlery on china.

As the meal continued, the conversation ebbed and flowed, punctuated by appreciative "mmms" and the occasional request to pass a dish. They were a tableau of satisfaction, a family forged not by blood but by circumstance and shared toil.

Once the meal began to wind down, Mick wiped

his lips and sat back. "So, are you guys ready to talk about what I discovered?"

"I thought you'd never ask," Sam said.

Jo started clearing plates. "Yeah, spill. We're dying to find out."

Mick leaned forward, his hands clasped in front of him on the table, the dim light from the overhead fixture casting deep shadows on his face. His voice was low but clear, a storyteller's cadence that held everyone rapt.

"I dug into the Duchamps—or the Woodsons, as they're known now," Mick began, his eyes scanning the faces around the table. "And there's a branch on that family tree that reaches right to the Websters."

Jo turned from the sink, her expression sharpening. Sam's chair creaked as he leaned in, his brow furrowed. They exchanged a knowing look.

"Ricky Webster keeps popping up in our investigations," Jo said.

"Ricky's just a kid, though," Sam interjected, his voice firm yet thoughtful. "Can't tie him to Tammy's case, not realistically."

Mick nodded in agreement. "Exactly, but family ties can be telling. It doesn't imply guilt but perhaps a path to explore."

The room seemed to hold its breath, awaiting the next piece of the puzzle.

"And there's more," Mick continued, reaching for his glass and swirling the liquid contemplatively before taking a sip. "April Summers? Well, she hasn't always been April Summers."

Bridget, who had been quietly refilling water glasses, paused. "Who was she?"

"She was Mary Madden not too long ago. Lived in White Rock. And she was married to Hank Madden."

Jo's eyes widened. "Hank Madden? Could that be H.M. from the day planner?"

"Could be. And if it is, then April's ex-husband might have been the last person to see her the day she died."

"That's not all," Mick said. "April or Mary also had ties to another person in town."

"Who?" Jo half-expected Mick to say Ricky Webster.

"Lily Dunn. She's her niece."

Jo was shocked. "You mean the artist?"

Mick shrugged. "I don't know who she is. Just have the name."

Jo glanced at Sam. "Maybe that's what Lily was hiding."

"And I can see why. Her bandana was found near there. But why would she lie?" Sam asked.

"Most liars I know are guilty of something," Holden said.

Sam nodded. "You got that right."

Jo looked around the room. "Well, that was enlightening on many fronts. Thanks, Mick." She gave a scrap of chicken to Lucy. "Eat good, girl, because we're going to have a busy day tomorrow."

CHAPTER TWENTY-THREE

The next morning, Jo and Sam went to visit Lily Dunn at her art studio. Wyatt had done some research on Hank Madden and found out he worked for one of the construction crews building a house up on mountain road. They decided to catch him when he got home later that afternoon instead of showing up at his work.

As Lucy, Sam, and Jo entered, the bell above the door announced their presence with a cheerful jingle.

Lily stood behind the counter, arranging a display of hand-painted mugs, her movements meticulous. Her smile was a thin veil over her anxiety as she greeted the detectives. "Back again, detectives? I hope you want to buy another painting."

Sam's eyes were gentle, but his voice carried a

weight that anchored the conversation in seriousness. "Not quite yet. We just need to ask you a few more questions."

Jo lingered near a stand with prints, her gaze not on the art but on Lily, reading the quivers of unease that ran through her.

"We wanted to ask about your aunt, Mary Madden," Sam said.

"Aunt Mary? I haven't heard from her in ages."

"When did you last hear from her?" Sam asked.

Lily's lips pursed. "It was before the divorce. She... she cut ties with us then. I haven't heard from her since."

Sam's gaze was steady, his voice carefully neutral as he broached the subject. "Did you know that your aunt had taken on a new identity? That she was going by the name April Summers?"

The question seemed to pierce through Lily's composure, her eyes widening as she shook her head slowly. "April Summers? No, I— What do you mean?"

Sam took a deep breath, readying himself to deliver the difficult news. "Your Aunt Mary had changed her name. We thought you might know why."

Lily's hands fluttered to her mouth, her eyes clouding with confusion and the beginning of distress.

"But... I had no idea. Why would she do that? Why wouldn't she tell us?"

"We're not sure yet," Jo added gently. "Sometimes people need a fresh start, or maybe there were other reasons. Unfortunately, she can't tell us herself."

Lily's grip tightened around the mug, a lifeline in the tumult of revelations. "I don't understand. Why can't she tell us?"

Sam leaned forward slightly, his voice as gentle as he could make it under the circumstances. "She was found dead at the owl sanctuary. Murdered."

The world seemed to tilt on its axis for Lily. She gripped the edge of the counter. "Murdered?" she whispered, a lone word filled with a chasm of realization and sorrow. "By who?"

"That's what we're trying to find out," Sam said, his voice firm, eyes locked on hers. "You surely can grasp how it looks. Your bandana was found not far from where your aunt was murdered."

Her reaction was instant. Her eyes ballooned in shock, and her posture stiffened. "You can't possibly believe I had anything to do with that! Why would I kill my aunt?"

"We're not accusing you," Sam clarified, but there was an edge of insistence in his tone. "We're just trying to piece together the puzzle. If there's anything you're holding back, now is the time."

Lily's façade began to crumble, the weight of implications and coincidences too heavy to bear in silence. "I—I was there but not for what you think. I was meeting someone."

"Who?" Sam asked.

Lily looked down at her feet. "It has nothing to do with my aunt."

"We'd still like to know," Sam insisted.

Lily nodded, a troubled frown creasing her brow. "Yes, but it was personal. We're... It's not something my parents approve of. I don't know anything about Aunt Mary being there or what happened to her, I swear."

"Lily," Sam said rather sharply. "Who were you meeting?"

"Ricky Webster."

Jo leaned in, a soft but authoritative presence. "You met with Ricky Webster near the sanctuary?"

"Yes, on Tuesday." Lily looked up at them, fear in her eyes. "I swear I never saw my aunt and have no idea what happened."

Sam was inclined to believe her, but maybe she was just a good actress. Still, he nodded slowly and passed her his card. "If you think of anything, let me know."

"I will." Lily nodded, looking relieved that they weren't putting her in cuffs and taking her into the station.

As they made their way to the car, the early morning stillness was beginning to give way to the buzz of the town waking up. Jo walked beside Sam, her strides matching his, the leash of their K-9, Lucy, looped loosely in her hand.

"Do you believe her?" Jo asked, her voice steady, her eyes scanning the street as they walked. "That she didn't know about her aunt being April?"

Sam paused by the driver's-side door of the Tahoe, glancing back at Lily's art shop, now quiet and unassuming in the light of day. "I'm not sure," he admitted. "But one thing's clear," he added as he unlocked the car and gestured for Lucy to jump in.

"And what's that?" Jo probed, her gaze following his.

"Ricky Webster lied to us," Sam said, his jaw setting firmly. "And we need to find out why."

CHAPTER TWENTY-FOUR

The Thorne construction site was a beehive of activity, with workers in hard hats and reflective vests moving about, their voices echoing over the noise of machinery. Dust kicked up around the soles of Sam and Jo's boots as they navigated through the organized chaos. Lucy was beside them, ears perked up and alert.

Ricky Webster was near the corner of the steel structure. His back was turned, and he was gesturing animatedly to a fellow worker, unaware of the approaching officers.

"Ricky Webster!" Sam called out, his voice firm enough to cut through the noise.

Ricky turned, his expression shifting from surprise to defiance as he recognized the uniformed figures.

A flicker of annoyance crossed his features, quickly masked by a feigned casual demeanor. He muttered something to his fellow workers before sauntering over to meet the pair.

Ricky's rough exterior softened for a moment as he extended his hand to pet Lucy, who, to Sam's surprise, wagged her tail in response. Ricky's eyes, wary yet defiant, met Sam's. "Can I help you, Chief?" he asked, his voice tinged with a forced politeness that didn't quite reach his eyes.

Sam noted the subtle shift in Ricky's posture—defensive yet trying to appear relaxed. He decided to cut straight to the chase. "Ricky, I think you might've forgotten to mention something important when we last talked," Sam began, his tone even but firm. "I wanted to give you another chance to come clean."

"Look, I already told you everything I know," Ricky started defensively before Sam cut him off.

"No, you didn't," Sam said, stepping closer. "You left out the part where you were with Lily Dunn near the owl sanctuary. Now I wonder, why would you lie about that?"

"It wasn't like that," Ricky insisted, his hands balled into fists at his sides. "I was just trying to keep Lily out of this mess. Her folks would be mad at her if they knew we were meeting."

"And what about her aunt?" Sam asked.

Ricky frowned. "Her aunt? I don't know her aunt."

Lucy's gaze flicked from Ricky to Sam. Her posture was relaxed. She didn't think Ricky was lying.

"You didn't know her aunt was April Summers?" Jo asked.

Ricky's brows shot up. "What? She never told me that."

"So you lied to keep her parents from knowing you were seeing each other? To protect her," Jo concluded, her tone skeptical but not unkind. "Or was it to protect yourself?"

"I've done nothing wrong!" Ricky's voice rose, tinged with anger and frustration.

Ricky's frustration was palpable as he crossed his arms defensively. "You're always accusing me," he blurted out, his tone laced with resentment. "But I never do anything wrong. Maybe you should stop wasting time on me and look at someone who actually had a problem with her."

Sam's interest piqued. Clearly, April Summers had been a figure of contention in the community, but Ricky's insinuation hinted at a specific conflict. "Who are you talking about, Ricky?" Sam asked, his voice calm but insistent.

Ricky's gaze shifted toward the construction

trailer, a temporary office amid the skeletal framework of the new build. He pointed a rough, work-worn finger in its direction. "Beryl Thorne," he said, his voice carrying a note of certainty. "I saw 'em—April and Beryl—arguing right over there."

Sam studied Ricky's expression, searching for any sign of deceit. "What were they arguing about?" he inquired, hoping for more detail.

Ricky shrugged, his expression one of frustration mixed with a hint of fear. "Dunno the words. Just heard shouting. But they were really going at it."

Sam glanced over at the trailer. Beryl said she hadn't known April. A wave of unease washed over him. If what Ricky said was true, Beryl had known April, and what an odd coincidence that it was Beryl who discovered the body.

Sam's gaze lingered on Ricky, weighing his words, the implications. "We'll talk to her," he assured. "But if we find out you're holding back more than you're letting on, protecting Lily will be the least of your worries."

As Sam and Jo stepped away from Ricky Webster, the wheels turned in Sam's head. How had Ricky, a construction worker, known April Summers, an activist who had seemingly come from nowhere?

"Ricky," Sam called out, spinning on his heel to

face the young man again. "One more thing—how did you know who April was?"

Ricky, who had started to turn back to his work, hesitated. He glanced over his shoulder, his posture stiffening. "Everyone who works in construction knew who she was after she started making trouble for the new development projects. Hard to miss someone when they're stirring up that much noise."

Sam nodded, satisfied for the moment. "All right, we'll be in touch if we have more questions."

As they walked away, Jo whispered to Sam, "Think he's telling the truth?"

Sam kept his eyes forward, watching Lucy sniff the ground. "Hard to say. But one thing's for sure. This case just got a lot more tangled."

CHAPTER TWENTY-FIVE

B eryl wasn't in the trailer, so Sam and Jo decided to head out to her house. Sam guided the Tahoe through the winding roads, the landscape awash with the vibrant hues of fall. The town's quaint, serene landscape belied the turmoil of the investigation they were entangled in. Lucy lay sprawled in the back seat, her ears occasionally twitching at the sound of their conversation.

Jo, sitting shotgun, gazed out at the passing scenery, her mind clearly elsewhere. She finally broke the silence, her voice tinged with skepticism. "I don't buy Beryl's innocent act, not for a second. It's too convenient, her stumbling upon the body the way she did."

Sam nodded, keeping his eyes on the road. He

knew of Jo's distrust toward Beryl. "You think she's involved?"

"I mean, she found April's body, right? And then there's the fight they had. Plus, her footprints all over the crime scene." Jo listed the points, ticking off each one with her fingers. "It's suspicious."

Lucy let out a soft whine from the back, as if in agreement. Sam glanced at her through the rearview mirror, a slight smile tugging at his lips. Lucy always had a sense for these things.

"But what about the larger man's footprint we found there? Could Beryl have had help?" Sam pondered, his tone contemplative.

Jo turned to face him, her brow furrowed. "An accomplice? Maybe. But then why show up the next day to 'discover' the body? A ploy to throw us off?"

Sam considered this. "It's possible. She's smart enough to think of that. But there's something that doesn't quite fit."

The Tahoe rolled past a charming row of local shops, their quaintness a stark contrast to the gravity of their conversation. Jo's gaze returned to the window, watching the world outside while her mind worked through the details of the case.

Jo shifted in her seat, her gaze still fixed on the passing scenery. "You know, the more I think about it, the more I can't shake off this feeling about the connection between the Websters and the Duchamps... or the Woodsons, as they're known now."

Sam glanced at her, his expression thoughtful. "It does seem like a strange coincidence."

"What are the odds that an old clue led me here and then we discover my old babysitter's family, who was investigated in Tammy's disappearance, moved here? They left town, changed their name, and now we find they're related to the Websters. Too many connections for it to be just a coincidence," Jo said, her voice tinged with a mix of suspicion and unresolved pain from her past.

Sam nodded slowly. "And we've had our run-ins with the Websters before. Remember the leads in that serial killer case that pointed to them? It turned out to be a dead end, but..."

"But it doesn't mean they're clean. Just that they weren't involved in that particular case," Jo interjected, her tone firm. "Ricky's too young to be a part of that, but his father or maybe an uncle... There's something there. I can feel it."

Lucy let out a soft huff from the back seat, almost as if in agreement. Sam reached over to give the dog a gentle pat. "We need to tread carefully. If there's a connection between the Woodsons and the Websters, it could lead to something much deeper."

Jo turned to face Sam, her eyes burning with a mix of determination and a deep-seated need for closure. "And more deadly."

Sam steered the cruiser onto a narrower road, the canopy of trees creating a dappled shade over them. "We'll look into the Woodsons' history deeper, that's for sure."

The conversation paused as they each retreated into their thoughts, piecing together the fragments of information. The car seemed to hum with the weight of their deliberations, Lucy's occasional shifts in the back seat the only sound breaking the silence.

Lucy shifted in the back, her movement drawing their attention. Jo reached back, giving the dog a reassuring pat. "Even Lucy's unsettled by this."

The Tahoe pulled into Beryl's driveway, the gravel crunching under its tires. Jo glanced at Sam, a determined look in her eyes. "Let's get some answers."

Sam nodded in agreement, killing the engine. Lucy perked up, sensing the shift in energy. The three of them stepped out of the car, ready to confront whatever lies awaited them inside.

"It's still hard to believe she stayed here after

everything with Lucas," Jo mused aloud, her gaze fixed on the mansion's towering façade.

Sam nodded in agreement. "Money and pride can make people cling to the strangest things."

Beryl greeted them with a performance of surprise and charm, her smile a little too wide, her eyes a little too bright. "Detectives! To what do I owe this pleasure?"

"We have a few questions," Sam said, his tone even.

Beryl ushered them into her living room, a space that radiated a false sense of warmth and comfort. Jo took in every detail—the perfectly placed cushions, the photographs smiling from the walls, the faint scent of lavender in the air. It all felt like a façade.

"So, Beryl, we need to talk about April Summers," Sam started, his voice steady.

Beryl's smile faltered slightly, but she quickly regained her composure. "April? I didn't know her, so I don't know what questions I could answer."

Jo observed Beryl's performance, a growing sense of disdain bubbling within her. She knew Beryl was lying, but Sam was playing along, giving Beryl enough rope.

"Are you sure about that, Beryl? Maybe you didn't

recognize her at first? Her face was covered, and you were understandably upset," Sam prodded gently.

Jo felt a flicker of annoyance. Sam was going too easy on her. Beryl, however, appeared to sense something was amiss. Her eyes narrowed slightly.

"What are you getting at, Sam?" Beryl's tone had a sharp edge.

Jo cut in before Sam could respond. "We know you're lying, Beryl. You were seen arguing with April."

Beryl's expression tightened. "Who told you that?"

"Our source is confidential," Jo stated firmly. "But they saw you, Beryl. Arguing with April, just days before she was found dead."

The room grew tense, the air thick with unspoken accusations and defensiveness. Beryl's façade of innocence began to crumble under the weight of their scrutiny.

"Fine," Beryl sighed, her composure breaking. "I knew her. We had... disagreements."

Sam leaned forward. "Disagreements about what, Beryl?"

Beryl's face twisted with disdain. "April was a snake, extorting money from me."

Sam leaned in, his voice even. "We heard she had a penchant for extortion."

"Worse," Beryl spat out. "She threatened to tell the

conservation committee that part of the land for the project was protected. Said she'd throw a wrench in the works."

Jo's eyes narrowed. "Is it protected land?"

Beryl shook her head vehemently. "No, but that's how despicable April was. She'd fabricate documents, make it look official, file a complaint. Get a judge to halt the construction... unless I paid her off. They'd eventually find out she was wrong, but in the meantime I'd lose a lot of money."

Jo absorbed this, her mind racing. "Is that why you killed her?"

Beryl recoiled as if struck. "I didn't kill anyone! I paid her to stop her lies."

Sam's gaze remained fixed on Beryl. "You understand how this looks, though? Your motive?"

"I understand," Beryl said, her voice a mixture of anger and fear. "That's why I said I didn't know her."

Jo's mind raced. Extortion. It was a motive, but was it the truth? Beryl's history of manipulation clouded the waters.

"Why didn't you tell us this before?" Jo demanded, her tone accusatory.

Beryl looked away, her hands clasping and unclasping in her lap. "I was scared."

Sam interjected, "And where were you the night of the murder, Beryl?"

Beryl turned to Sam, a wounded look in her eye. "Seriously? You think I had something to do with her death?"

"Your footprints were at the scene. You had an argument with her. You lied to us. You even discovered the body." Sam spread his hands. "I'm going to need more than your word."

Beryl sat straighter. "If you must know, I was out with someone all night."

Sam's left brow quirked. "So you have an alibi? Mind telling us who it is so we can check it?"

Beryl looked away from Sam. "Victor Sorentino."

Jo glanced at Sam. Victor? That smooth-suited guy they'd met at the owl protest? He was a bigwig at Convale. Jo wondered how Beryl knew him. Clearly, they had a relationship close enough for her to spend the night. Sam didn't seem at all bothered by that, which was a good sign. It was clear Beryl had a thing for Sam, and at one time Jo had thought maybe Sam returned her affections. Jo was relieved to see that wasn't the case.

Sam noted it down. "We'll need to confirm that."

"Fine," Beryl said. "Is there anything else?"

Sam rose. "I think that's it for now. Thanks for your time."

They stepped outside, the chill air a sharp contrast to the stifling atmosphere of Beryl's living room. Jo took a deep breath, trying to shake off the claustrophobia.

"Do you think she's telling the truth?" Jo asked.

Sam shrugged. "Maybe. We'll check her alibi. See what Victor has to say."

They got into the Tahoe, each with their own thoughts. They'd left Lucy in the car with the windows cracked, and the dog, sensing the mood, lay quietly in the back seat, her presence a silent support in the sea of uncertainties they navigated.

CHAPTER TWENTY-SIX

Kevin sat in the dim light of his living room, the glow from his laptop casting shadows across his face. The thumb drive, an unassuming piece of plastic and metal, lay next to the printout of the pictures he'd taken of the notebook he'd found in the evidence room. He'd poured over the pages, deciphering the cryptic notes scrawled in the margins. Each set of numbers and words he tried from the notebook felt like a key, but so far, none had fit the lock.

With a deep breath, Kevin tried another combination from the notebook, his fingers tapping the keys with a mix of hope and skepticism. The screen blinked —access denied, again. He rubbed his temples, feeling the weight of frustration and the nagging sense that the answer was right there, just out of reach.

Then a sequence of numbers and a word written in the corner of a page caught his eye. They were different, less orderly, almost an afterthought. It was a strange combination, but something about it felt right. With a hesitant hand, Kevin entered the sequence into the password prompt.

The moment he pressed Enter, the folder icon changed, signaling success. He leaned in closer, his heart rate quickening. The contents of the drive began to reveal themselves—about a dozen images, each featuring a grove of beech trees.

Kevin scrolled through them, a mix of disbelief and realization dawning on him. This was very strange. The lower branches didn't look natural. It was as if someone had broken and stripped them as some sort of marker.

"What does this have to do with the narcotics case?" he wondered aloud. The notebook, the thumb drive, the trees—there was a link, a mystery wrapped in the shadows of his own lost memories.

His eyes fixed on a set of numbers. Coordinates? Whatever these trees signified, they were a bread-crumb trail leading to answers he desperately needed to find.

Kevin's initial surge of excitement ebbed away,

replaced by a creeping sense of puzzlement. This wasn't the incriminating evidence or dangerous secrets he had anticipated. It was... benign, almost disappointingly so. But then again, in a town like theirs, where every detail could mean something more, Kevin couldn't shake off the feeling that these pictures, these markings, held a significance he couldn't yet understand.

He thought about the branches, wondering if they were some sort of code or message. The numbers, too, intrigued him. Could they be locations? And if so, what did they signify? A meeting place or perhaps somewhere that drugs or drug money had been stashed? It was a puzzle, but not the kind he expected to find.

With a sigh, Kevin decided it was time to bring someone else in. Sam would know what to do, he thought. He would hand over the drive to him when he visited the station next. Perhaps together, they could unravel this peculiar mystery.

But how would he explain cracking the code? Just luck? He couldn't tell Sam he'd taken pictures of the notebook in evidence. That was against the rules, and he didn't want anything to jeopardize his chances of full reinstatement.

As he shut down his laptop, Kevin couldn't help but feel a mix of worry and curiosity. The discovery felt significant yet elusive, a piece of a larger puzzle he was yet to see in its entirety.

CHAPTER TWENTY-SEVEN

"Looks like Jamison didn't waste any time." Jo pointed to the campaign sign with Jamison's name in bold letters. He'd put it on the opposite side of the walkway from Marnie's in front of the police station.

"I hope this doesn't turn into a sign war in front of the station." Sam opened the door and gestured for Jo and Lucy to enter.

Inside, Reese was crouched on the floor in the corner, meticulously applying the last strokes of paint to the baseboard. Lucy rushed over, whining slightly.

"Don't worry. I'm fine!" Reese laughed, patting Lucy's head, amused by her apparent concern.

Reese stood up, wiping her hands on a rag.

"Almost done in here. Planning to start on the hallway next, if that's okay with you, Sam."

Sam looked around, nodding. "It's looking good, Reese. Go ahead with the hallway."

The front door of the station opened, and in walked Harry Woolston. Now pushing eighty, Harry had once been the chief of police, and he loved to stop by to talk about old times. He was somewhat of a mentor to Sam, so his presence was always welcome even though Sam did sometimes get frustrated with Harry's habit of trying to "help" with the cases.

"Evening, everyone," Harry greeted, his voice deep and resonant. He glanced around, taking in the fresh coat of paint with a nod of approval. "Sprucing up the place, I see. I don't think this place has been painted since I was chief."

Sam stepped forward to greet him. "Harry, always good to see you. What brings you by?"

Harry, removing his hat, revealed his shock of white hair and characteristic warm, yet shrewd, eyes. "Just passing by and thought I'd drop in. Saw that campaign sign out front, Sam. Supporting Marnie for mayor, are you?"

Sam shifted slightly, a touch of discomfort in his stance. "Marnie thought our station was prime real estate for her sign. I'm staying neutral, though. As you can see, Jamison has put his stake in the ground too."

Harry chuckled, seemingly unfazed by Sam's diplomatic response. "Of course, of course. So, how's the April Summers case going?"

"We're running down some leads," Sam said.

Harry laughed and petted Lucy. "I know that means you aren't narrowing in on anyone."

Sam smiled. "Don't be too sure. We have several suspects."

"Funny thing it is, that she changed her name and all," Harry said. "I knew her when she was Mary Madden. She seemed like a nice girl."

"It sounds like she wasn't very nice as April Summers." Jo held up a coffee mug to offer Harry a cup.

Harry shook his head. "Gotta watch my caffeine after three p.m."

"So do you know anyone who would want her dead?" Sam asked.

Harry shook his head. "Nah, didn't know her well. I remember the divorce. It was quiet. No violence or fighting like you get these days. Things seem so much more violent. Like, look at all the murders. Never had that many in my day."

Sam laughed. "Guess things were a lot better back then."

Harry leaned against the counter, his eyes reflecting a time long past. "Sure were. You know, though, I remember another person who changed their name. A whole family, actually."

Jo looked up from her coffee. Was he talking about the Woodsons? She'd never considered that Harry might be able to shed some light on her sister's case. "You do?"

"Oh, they were a curious case. Moved to town about thirty years ago under the name Woodson. Had a bit of trouble with their boy once, and when I dug deeper, I found they'd changed their name. A strange coincidence, don't you think?"

Sam glanced at Jo and asked, "What was the trouble with their son?"

"Nothing serious, just some teenage rebellion. But it involved Daniel Webster. That man was always a bit of a troublemaker. I remember pulling in Barry Woodson and Webster for questioning over some petty theft."

Jo, her detective instincts kicking in, took note. "Who is Daniel Webster? Is he related to Ricky?"

Harry nodded. "His uncle."

"What kind of troublemaker was he?"

Harry scrunched up his face. "Stealing, B and E, nothing too bad."

Jo thought there was a big difference between these small crimes and being a child abductor or serial killer. Still, Jo made a mental note to find out more about this uncle.

Harry's phone pinged, and he took it from his pocket, squinting. A look of alarm crossed his face. "Uh-oh. Looks like the missus needs me to bring some milk home for supper. Guess I lost track of time."

Sam thanked Harry for stopping by, and Harry left in a rush.

"Boy, his wife really has tightened the leash on him," Reese said.

Jo laughed. "It was interesting he remembered that old case with the Websters and Woodsons. I just keep thinking there is something there."

"Me too. But right now, I think it's about time we go question Hank Madden. He should be home from work by now." Sam turned back toward the door.

They stepped out of the station, the evening air crisp and cool. The town seemed peaceful, but Jo knew that under the calm surface, there were undercurrents of turmoil. They were getting close.

In the car, Jo turned to Sam. "Harry's visit was timely. I think we need to find more about the

Websters for Tammy's case. Ricky and Hazel are pretty tight-lipped, but I bet we can get something out of Lily. Seems like it would be easy to get her to talk."

Sam nodded. "I agree, but first let's see what Hank Madden has to say."

CHAPTER TWENTY-EIGHT

The Tahoe pulled up to a modest, weathered house, a stark contrast to the grandeur of Beryl's residence. Sam, Jo, and Lucy got out and approached the door, seeing a shadow peek out through a side window as they walked toward the front steps. They were surprised when the door swung open to reveal Danika Ryder, the woman from the logging area, her face etched with worry.

"Detectives? What brings you here?" she asked, her voice tinged with nervousness.

"We're here to see Hank Madden," Sam stated, his tone professional yet firm.

Danika looked relieved. Had she thought they were here for her? Then she hesitated, eyeing the detectives with a mix of curiosity and apprehension. "I was just getting ready to go to work. I had the morning off. Does this have anything to do with what you were questioning Travis about out at the logging site?" she asked cautiously, referencing their previous visit.

Sam, maintaining a neutral expression, replied, "We really just need to talk to Hank. Don't let us keep you from getting to work. Though it is an interesting coincidence, finding you here."

Danika shifted her weight, a flicker of concern crossing her features. "Well, I live here," she explained, as if to justify her presence. "With Hank."

Just then, Hank appeared beside her, his expression a blend of surprise and wariness.

"Detectives? What's this about?" he inquired, his expression shifting from surprise to guarded caution upon seeing them. Lucy sniffed the air, sensing the tension.

Sam wasted no time. "Mr. Madden, I'm Chief Mason, and this is Sergeant Harris. Could we come in?"

Apprehension crossed Hank's face, but he nodded and opened the door for them to enter. The living room, into which they stepped, was a stark contrast to the unassuming exterior of the house. It was unexpectedly spacious and neatly kept, yet there was an air of simplicity to it.

The walls were adorned with a few framed photographs, capturing what seemed like happier times—a younger Hank with friends, a few hunting trophies, and scenic landscapes. The furniture was modest but comfortable, an older-style sofa and matching armchairs arranged around a well-worn coffee table.

Hank stood to the side and motioned for them to sit.

"This won't take long," Sam said and remained standing. Lucy stood beside him, her nose twitching as she took in a variety of smells that were undetectable to Sam.

"You were married to Mary Madden, is that right?" Sam asked.

Hank crossed his arms over his chest. "Yes. That was a long time ago, though."

"Were you aware that she changed her name to April Summers?"

Hank's eyes flickered with a mixture of recognition and discomfort. "Yes, I was aware. Toward the end of our marriage, Mary... She started changing. It was one of the reasons we couldn't make it work."

Jo observed him closely, noting the mix of resignation and bitterness in his tone. "Changed how?" she probed.

"She became distant, secretive. Like she was becoming someone else. When I heard she changed her name, I wasn't surprised," Hank admitted, his gaze drifting momentarily.

Sam turned to Danika. She didn't look at all surprised to hear this news. "Did you know that Hank had been married to April Summers?"

Danika nodded.

"And you didn't think to mention that when we were at the logging site the other day?" Sam asked.

"I didn't think it was relevant. You were questioning Travis about April's escapades with the tree. That has nothing to do with us." Danika gestured from herself to Hank.

Sam stared at Danika for a few beats. It made her nervous, judging by the way her eyes darted from Sam to Hank.

He turned back to Hank. "Are you aware that April Summers was murdered?"

Hank nodded. "Danika told me you were out at the logging site the other day."

"After the divorce, did you keep in touch with her?" Sam leaned slightly forward to gauge Hank's reaction.

"Hardly. We went our separate ways. I had little to

do with her once she became April," Hank asserted, but his voice lacked conviction.

Danika stood close to Hank, her body language protective.

Sam pressed on. "Your initials were in April's day planner. A meeting scheduled for the night she died. Can you explain that?"

Hank's eyes darted to Danika, a flicker of panic crossing his face. "My initials? I never had a meeting with her. Maybe it was someone else with the same initials."

Sam had to admit that could be true, but he didn't think that was the case.

"Are you sure you didn't talk to her? Did she call? Maybe you ran into her in the store and she wanted to meet, and you said yes just to appease her?" Jo suggested, just in case Hank didn't want to admit to meeting his ex in front of Danika.

Danika quickly chimed in. "He couldn't have met her. We were together here, at home, all night that night."

Hank frowned at Danika. "Yes, that's right. I usually don't go out much on work nights. My job is too physically demanding, and I need lots of sleep."

Jo's eyes narrowed. Something seemed off about

their alibi. She glanced at Lucy, who let out a low, rumbling growl, echoing the detectives' skepticism.

Sam continued. "We'll need to verify that alibi. Do you have anyone who can confirm you were both here?"

Hank shifted uncomfortably. "It was just us," he muttered, avoiding direct eye contact.

As they left Hank's house, the evening air had a crispness to it, a reminder that the day was drawing to a close. Jo mulled over the conversation, her instincts telling her there was more to Hank and Danika's story.

Jo began, "That alibi is a little too convenient."

Sam nodded in agreement. "We need to check their story. There's more to this than Hank's letting on."

"Maybe we should swing back after Danika goes to work." Jo opened the back door, and Lucy jumped in, then she got into the passenger seat.

Sam nodded in agreement, starting the car. "It's a strange coincidence, her showing up twice in this case. Something doesn't add up. And why didn't she mention she was living with April's ex when we were questioning Travis?"

"Let's not forget there's still Beryl," Jo added. "My money's still on her being involved."

"I need to check with Sorentino about her alibi." Sam's lips pursed as if the very thought was distasteful.

Jo glanced at the clock. It was nearing five p.m.—an opportune time to catch Lily at her shop. "I'd like to talk to Lily again to see if she can tell us more about the Websters. I have a hunch they are involved in my sister's case. The shop should be quiet around this time, and I feel like she might open up to me."

Sam gave a nod of approval. "Good idea. I'll go up to Convale and have a talk with Sorentino."

"Sounds like a plan," Jo said, a determined glint in her eye.

Sam pulled into the station, and Jo hopped out and headed toward their other official car, an old model Crown Victoria. "I'll see you back here in about an hour."

"See you then." Sam pulled back onto the road and headed toward the Convale Corporate office.

CHAPTER TWENTY-NINE

Kevin walked into the station, the thumb drive a small but significant weight in his pocket. He'd been second-guessing himself about turning it in. It felt almost like a burden, and he wished he had someone he could trust, someone he could talk it over with. But he didn't. He could only trust himself.

He immediately noticed the freshly painted walls and Reese, diligently adding the final touches. At a nearby desk, Wyatt was engrossed in something on his computer.

"Place is looking good," Kevin commented, glancing around.

Reese looked up, her face breaking into a smile. "Thanks, Kevin. I'm pretty happy with the progress."

Major meandered over to Kevin, rubbing against

his leg. He bent down to give the cat a scratch behind the ears. "Hey, buddy."

Wyatt chimed in without looking up from his screen. "What's up, Kev? You finally coming back full time?"

"Not yet," Kevin replied, his hand still on Major. "Hopefully soon, though. Where's Sam and Jo?"

Reese dipped her brush in the paint. "Last I saw, Sam dropped Jo off, and then they both headed out again. Must've gotten some leads. They were coming back from questioning Hank Madden but didn't come into the station."

Kevin nodded. "How's the case going?"

"It's still in the narrowing-down stage, but at least the leads haven't dried up. You heard about how April used to be Mary Madden, right?" Wyatt asked.

Kevin nodded.

"And Beryl Thorne lied about not knowing her," Reese added. "I wouldn't be surprised if she was behind this."

Both Kevin and Wyatt snorted.

"No kidding. She's not to be trusted," Kevin said.

"We could use you back here, Kevin," Wyatt said sincerely, finally looking up from his computer. "Place isn't the same without you."

"Yeah, we miss having you around," Reese added,

a sentiment of genuine camaraderie in her voice. "Seems like things are moving in the right direction. I mean, you did get to go out and settle the issue with Nettie and Rita, so that's progress."

Kevin laughed, the warmth of their words giving him a sense of belonging. Hopefully giving the thumb drive to Sam would help solidify his standing as part of the team but not if he told Sam how he'd cracked it. Instead, he'd just pretend like he'd gotten lucky with the passwords.

Part of him hesitated at that. If he didn't tell anyone that the password had been found in the notebook related to that narcotics case, that could be withholding evidence. It would probably get sorted out, though, once someone figured out what those images were for. Kevin was sure it would come back around, and if it was an important part of that case, someone would figure it out. Or maybe he should pretend that he hadn't been able to crack it at all.

"I hope I'm not stuck only dealing with Nettie and Rita when I get back. I'd like to think my talents are best used elsewhere."

After a few more minutes of conversation, Kevin checked his watch. "I should head out. I hope you guys catch a break in the investigation."

"Thanks," Wyatt said, returning to his typing.

"See you Monday," Reese called as Kevin walked out the door. Monday was the next day that Kevin was due back to work. He guessed he could give the thumb drive to Sam then. That would give him time to decide if he wanted to let Sam know he'd figured out the password or not.

It was a short walk to the town diner. The interior was a cozy blend of classic and modern—checkerboard floors paired with sleek, comfortable booths and warm, ambient lighting. The walls were adorned with black-and-white photos of the town's history, adding a touch of nostalgia.

He chose a booth near the window, sliding into the cushioned seat with a view of the street. The waitress, who had a friendly face with a ready smile, came over almost immediately. "What can I get for you, hon?"

"Coffee, black, and a piece of apple pie, please," Kevin ordered, settling into the comforting rhythm of the diner.

As she bustled away, Kevin's hand brushed against the thumb drive in his pocket. He leaned back, his gaze drifting outside, lost in thought.

The diner was the polar opposite of the seedy one where he had seen Bridget—clean, well lit, a place where families and friends gathered. The memory of Bridget flashed in his mind. Despite their brief interactions, he felt a connection to her, a sense of trust that he couldn't quite explain.

The waitress returned with his coffee and pie, the aroma of the freshly baked apple filling the air around him. "Here you go. Let me know if you need anything else," she said warmly.

"Thanks," Kevin replied, offering a grateful smile. He took a sip of the hot coffee, letting the bitterness and warmth ground him in the moment.

Kevin's thoughts were interrupted as the diner door swung open, a familiar figure stepping inside. Bridget, as if summoned by his musings, appeared, her eyes scanning the room before landing on him. Her eyes widened in surprise, and a small smile played on her lips as she made her way over.

"Seems like we're destined to keep bumping into each other in diners," Bridget joked, her voice light.

Kevin chuckled, shifting in his seat to face her. "Can't help it. I'm a fan of good food and coffee," he replied with an easy grin. "Care to join me? I promise I'm not stalking you with diner locations."

Bridget laughed, the sound warm and genuine. "I'd love to," she said, sliding into the seat opposite him. "I was just thinking I could use a good cup of coffee."

The waitress came over, and Bridget ordered a coffee, her eyes twinkling with amusement as she looked back at Kevin. "So, what brings you here today? Other than the obvious culinary delights, of course."

Kevin, feeling a pleasant flutter of happiness at her company, leaned back, enjoying the moment. He knew he should keep things light. Small talk. He hardly knew her. But as he talked about the weather, the urge to tell her about the thumb drive and his worries about it being something really important gnawed at him.

CHAPTER THIRTY

There were no customers milling about in Dunn Art, just the way Jo had hoped. Lily was in the back corner arranging a large canvas, and Jo stepped in quietly. The air was thick with the scent of paint and varnish, a sharp contrast to the crisp autumn air outside. As Jo approached, Lily looked up, her eyes flickering with a hint of anxiety.

"Sergeant Harris," Lily greeted, her voice slightly tremulous. "What brings you back?"

Jo took a seat on one of the wooden stools near the counter. "I have a few more questions about Ricky Webster," she said, watching Lily closely.

Lily's hands paused in their work, and she let out a small sigh. "What about him?"

"It's about his family, actually," Jo clarified. "I'm

interested in his father and uncle. What can you tell me about them?"

Lily hesitated, glancing toward the door as if expecting someone. "I don't know much about them. He mentioned his uncle was sort of a black sheep. Been in and out of jail a few times."

"And Ricky?" Jo probed gently.

"He's different," Lily defended quickly. "He's not like them."

Jo nodded, noting the defensiveness in Lily's tone. "Do you know if Ricky ever mentioned anything about his father or uncle that struck you as odd or concerning?"

Lily frowned. "Odd or concerning? What do you mean?"

"You know, like something out of the ordinary."

Lily chewed her lip, clearly conflicted. "Not really. Ricky doesn't talk much about his family. He tries to keep his distance from that side of his life. Well, except his grandmother. He dotes on her."

Lily's hands moved to a gold chain around her neck, fidgeting nervously. Jo noticed that she wasn't wearing her usual bandana today. "How well do you know Ricky's family?"

"I don't," Lily admitted. "But his grandmother, Hazel, she's... kind of eccentric."

Jo pondered this, her mind racing. "And Ricky, has he ever shown any violent tendencies?"

Lily's eyes widened. "No, nothing like that. He's a good person, just... misunderstood."

Jo observed Lily's increasing agitation. "Lily, you seem nervous. Is there something you're not telling me?"

Lily shook her head, her voice barely above a whisper. "I just... I don't want to cause any trouble for Ricky."

Jo softened her tone. "I understand. But anything you tell me could help. Has Ricky ever mentioned anything about his family's past?"

"Ricky's always kept his distance from his family's troubles. He tries to stay out of it." Lily's eyes narrowed. "Do you think someone in his family did something to Aunt Mary... I mean, April? I don't think they even knew her."

"Maybe not as Mary, but you yourself admitted you didn't know anything about her once she was April Summers." Jo didn't want to tell Lily she was really asking because she suspected the Websters had something to do with her sister Tammy.

Lily nodded slowly, her gaze drifting as if lost in thought. "Ricky mentioned some trouble down in another state... Pennsylvania, I think. Is that where Aunt Mary went after she left here?"

Jo's mind clicked into place. Pennsylvania was indeed one of the addresses linked to April Summers. "Yes, she was there."

Lily's eyes flitted around the empty shop. Her voice lowered, and she leaned closer. "His uncle got into some trouble there. Some bad business."

Jo's pulse quickened. A previous serial killer case she'd looked into involving children had been in Pennsylvania. "And Ricky's father?"

Lily bit her lip, clearly uncomfortable. "Like I said, I really don't know anything about him."

As they spoke, Lily's fingers nervously twisted the gold chain around her neck. Then, as Lily adjusted her top, the necklace slipped out, revealing a crystal ball pendant. Jo's heart stopped for a moment. The pendant was identical to one her mother had worn, the one Tammy used to love.

"That necklace," Jo said, her voice steady despite the shock. "Where did you get it?"

Lily glanced down, seemingly surprised by its appearance. "Oh, this? Ricky gave it to me. He said it was special."

Jo felt a surge of adrenaline, and she reached out to touch the crystal. Running her thumb over the surface, she felt a rough spot. Images of her mother inspecting it and announcing it just had a small chip after Tammy dropped it bubbled up.

Lily stepped back, looking a bit alarmed at the way Jo had grabbed the necklace, but Jo continued, "Ricky gave this to you? Do you know where he got it?"

Lily shook her head. "He never said. Just that it was from his family. Like an heirloom or something."

Jo's mind raced, piecing together the puzzle. The connection between the Websters and her family's past was too strong to be a coincidence. She stood abruptly.

"Lily, thank you. You've been more helpful than you know."

As Jo hurried out of the shop, her thoughts were a whirlwind. She needed to get to the Webster house. If Ricky's father or uncle had ties to her family's past, especially to Tammy's disappearance, she had to uncover the truth. Jo's heart pounded as she rushed to her car. She should tell Sam, Bridget, and Holden, but every second counted. She was close to finding out the truth, and nothing was going to stop her.

CHAPTER THIRTY-ONE

The Convale corporate offices were set deep in the woods on the outskirts of town. A symbol of corporate might, the building loomed over the small town, its sleek glass façade reflecting the afternoon sun. Sam's grip on the steering wheel tightened, the company's plans to industrialize White Rock's pristine lands grating against his love for the town's natural beauty.

Parking the cruiser, he took a moment to compose himself. Convale, with its giant energy structures, threatened to change the town forever, and Victor Sorentino was the face of that change. Sam's previous encounter with Victor had left a lasting impression. The man was polished, urbane, a stark contrast to the rugged simplicity of White Rock.

He reached into the back seat, unclipping Lucy's seat belt. She jumped out, her tail wagging, always ready for action.

Sam liked bringing Lucy along when he questioned people. She was more than just a police K-9. She was a keen judge of character. Her reactions to people often gave Sam valuable insights, and her presence tended to unnerve those he questioned, making it easier to extract information. Besides, no one ever questioned the chief of police bringing a K-9 along, even in places where animals weren't typically allowed.

"I don't really like this Sorentino guy," Sam muttered to Lucy as they approached the sleek glass doors of the building. He thought back to his previous encounter with Victor Sorentino. There was something about the man he didn't trust. His demeanor was too polished, too controlled. It was almost as if he was performing.

Lucy looked up at Sam, her whiskey-brown eyes full of agreement. Sam knew Lucy felt the same as he did.

Stepping into the lobby, Sam passed by a large model of an energy structure, a reminder of what was at stake. He approached the receptionist, who eyed Lucy warily as the K-9 sniffed around, her senses alert.

"I'm here to see Victor Sorentino," Sam announced, his tone carrying an edge of authority.

"Do you have an appointment?" the women asked.

Sam smiled and pointed to his badge. "No, but I'm pretty sure he'll make time to see me."

The receptionist made a call, her eyes flicking to Sam and then to Lucy. "Mr. Sorentino will see you now," she said, directing him to the elevators.

Victor's office was on the top floor, offering a panoramic view of the town and the unspoiled forest around it. Unspoiled for now, Sam thought, because if Convale had its way, there would be an ugly path of giant metal electrical towers slashing through the landscape.

The office was spacious and impeccably decorated in a sleek, modern style. Victor stood by the window, his back to Sam, gazing out over the town. His dark hair caught the light, and his posture exuded a sense of command.

Victor turned and greeted them with a polished smile, though his eyes betrayed a hint of curiosity at Lucy's presence.

"Chief Mason," Victor began, extending his hand in greeting. "To what do I owe this unexpected visit?"

Sam shook Victor's hand, maintaining a steady gaze. "I'm following up on some leads in the April

Summers case," he said, watching for Victor's reaction.

Victor raised an eyebrow, his composure intact. "April Summers? I'm afraid I don't see how that would involve me." He moved to sit on the leather chair behind his desk and gestured for Sam to sit on the chair facing it.

"That's what I'm here to find out," Sam replied evenly. "Did you know April?"

Victor's response was swift and smooth. "No, I can't say that I did. What would my connection to her be?"

Sam observed Victor carefully. "One of our suspects claimed you were their alibi for the night April was killed."

The surprise on Victor's face seemed genuine. "An alibi? For whom?"

"Beryl Thorne," Sam stated. "She mentioned she was with you that evening."

Victor paused, his expression shifting as he processed the information. "Ah, Beryl," he said after a moment. "Yes, we had a late dinner, and she came back to my place."

Sam nodded, noting the slight delay in Victor's recognition. "Can anyone else corroborate that?"

Victor leaned back in his chair, a confident air returning to him. "I'm sure the staff at the restaurant can vouch for our meeting, but as for my place, it was just the two of us. She did stay until morning, but she left before dawn to get some early morning pictures at the owl sanctuary."

Victor had a bit of a smirk on his face as he said that, and Lucy let out a sniff. Sam imagined that was the dog's version of rolling her eyes.

Sam leaned forward slightly, maintaining a casual tone. "Word around town is that April had a penchant for extortion. Did she ever try that with Convale?"

Victor's expression remained unfazed. "Extortion? If she did, it never reached my desk. Convale is a large company, Detective. We deal with all sorts of allegations and claims."

Sam nodded, filing away Victor's response. "How well did Beryl know April? Did she ever mention having an argument with her that day?"

Victor paused, his eyes narrowing briefly. "No, she didn't mention any argument. Why would she?"

"That's interesting," Sam mused. "You had dinner together that night. I would think Beryl might want to vent about an argument with someone she knew."

Victor shrugged, a dismissive gesture. "Our conversation was primarily about business... and other things."

"And what other things would those be, if you don't mind me asking?" Sam probed, watching Victor's reaction closely.

Victor let out a laugh, though it lacked warmth. "Personal stuff. Nothing pertinent to your investigation, I assure you."

Victor leaned forward, fixing Sam with a scrutinizing gaze. "You seem quite interested in Beryl, Detective. Is there something I should be aware of regarding you two?"

Sam met Victor's gaze steadily. "No, there's nothing. Just following up on all leads."

As the interview concluded, Victor stood up, his posture relaxed yet authoritative. "Is there anything else, Detective?"

Sam took a moment then shook his head. "Not for now."

Leaving Victor's office, Sam went over the interview in his head. Could Victor and Beryl have teamed up to kill April? Victor seemed like the type of guy who would have someone else do his dirty work, but that didn't mean he wasn't involved somehow. But why would they kill her?

In the car, Sam turned to Lucy in the back seat. "I still don't like him, do you?"

Lucy gave a soft woof, indicating that she still didn't like Victor either.

CHAPTER THIRTY-TWO

Jo's gaze swept over the dilapidated old farmhouse as she approached. It was the only house for miles, standing isolated, far from town, a testament to neglect and years of wear. The screen door, its mesh hanging out like an afterthought, creaked eerily in the wind.

She rapped on the wooden frame, her heart pounding with a mix of determination and apprehension. Hazel Webster, a lit cigarette dangling from her lips, answered the door. Her eyes, sharp and defensive, sized Jo up.

"Well, if it isn't White Rock's finest," Hazel declared, her voice a rasp of suspicion.

"Is Ricky home?" Jo would much rather discuss this with Ricky than Hazel. Even though Hazel probably knew more about the past, Jo didn't trust her answers.

"Nope." Hazel started to shut the door.

"I'm here to talk about a necklace," Jo said hastily. "A crystal ball pendant. Ricky gave it to Lily Dunn."

Hazel's eyes narrowed, and she looked at Jo, opening the door a smidge wider. "Accusing my grandson of stealing now, are you? Ricky's a good boy. Don't you forget that."

"No, no," Jo quickly reassured her. "We think it's important to a case. We know Ricky didn't steal it. Actually, it was some sort of family heirloom."

The mention of a family heirloom seemed to trigger something in Hazel. Her fierce demeanor wavered, replaced by a flicker of curiosity. "Heirloom, you say?"

Jo nodded, describing the unique pendant in detail. A spark appeared behind Hazel's bloodshot eyes. She knew something.

"Maybe I remember something. Come in," Hazel muttered, turning back into the shadows of the house.

Hesitation gripped Jo. She should let Sam know what was going on. But Hazel had already disappeared inside, and if she wanted more answers, she'd have to follow. Besides, Hazel was a frail old woman, nothing for Jo to be afraid of.

Taking a deep breath, Jo stepped over the threshold into the dimly lit interior that seemed to swallow light whole.

The house smelled of stale smoke and old wood. Dust motes danced in the slivers of light filtering through dirty windows. Jo followed Hazel through a narrow hallway lined with crooked family photos, each frame holding a faded memory.

They entered a cluttered living room, where Hazel gestured to a worn sofa. The house was oppressive from the water stains creeping down the walls to the old worn fabric on the furniture. She felt sorry for Ricky living here.

As Hazel settled into an armchair, her eyes became distant, her words slow and measured. "Now, what's this about a necklace?" Hazel's voice trailed off, her eyes suddenly snapping back to the present. She looked at Jo with a new intensity, as if weighing whether to reveal more.

"It was a crystal necklace, the kind that reflects a rainbow of light. Do you know where it came from?" Jo asked.

Hazel took a long drag of her cigarette, the ember glowing in the gloom. Jo suppressed the urge to cough.

The silence stretched, thick with anticipation. Jo leaned forward, sensing the importance of what

Hazel might disclose next. The old house creaked around them, as if echoing the tension of the moment.

Hazel's demeanor transformed as a sharp, knowing glint appeared in her eyes. She leaned forward, scrutinizing Jo with an intensity that hadn't been there moments before. "My sister-in-law had a necklace like that," she said, her voice carrying a weight that made the air in the room feel heavier.

Jo shifted uncomfortably, feeling a chill run down her spine. "And where is your sister-in-law now?" she replied cautiously.

Hazel chuckled, a low, raspy sound that echoed slightly in the cluttered room. "Long gone. We were close once after she moved here. Sad thing what happened."

"What happened?" Jo asked.

Hazel got that glazed look again. "There was a tragedy near their home." Hazel shook her head. "They had to move away. The police had been poking around, and my brother-in-law, well... he wasn't quite right."

Jo's gut churned. "Did they move up here?"

Hazel nodded.

"The Woodsons," Jo said.

Hazel looked at her sharply. "How did you know?

Is this related to that April Summers incident? Ricky had nothing to do with any of it."

"I know," Jo reassured her. The last thing she wanted was for Hazel to get mad and kick her out. Not when it seemed like she was going to finally get some answers. But could she trust Hazel's answers? The woman was clearly not all there.

An ominous creak from down the hall captured Jo's attention, drawing her gaze toward the shadowed entrance of another room. A fleeting glimpse of what seemed like an arm resting on a chair sparked her curiosity. Was someone else in the house, silently observing their conversation?

Hazel, noticing Jo's diverted focus, commented casually, "Oh, that's just the dining room. That's where we usually have our tea. In fact, I seem to have lost my manners. I should have asked if you'd like some."

Jo couldn't shake off a creeping sense of unease. She didn't want to stay for tea, but her detective instincts urged her to maintain a façade of normalcy if she hoped to get more answers from Hazel.

"Tea sounds lovely," she said, her voice steady despite the racing thoughts.

Hazel nodded, her movements slow but deliberate. "You stay right here," she commanded, her tone leaving no room for argument as she shuffled off to the kitchen.

Once Hazel's footsteps faded, Jo seized the opportunity to investigate. She tiptoed toward the dining room, her heart pounding with a mix of anticipation and dread. Was someone in there listening, and what would they do if she appeared in the doorway?

She inched closer. There was someone in a chair... or something. She could see an arm, but it was oddly still.

"Here's your tea." Hazel's voice in her ear made her jump.

Jo whirled around to see Hazel standing with a flower-patterned china teacup and saucer extended toward Jo. How had the women snuck up on her without Jo hearing?

"We'll take it in the living room." Hazel herded Jo back to the other room, and they sat. Jo took a few sips of tea to be polite.

Jo leaned forward, her focus sharpened. "Can you tell me more about your brother-in-law? What was the specific issue?"

Hazel's gaze turned piercing, almost knowing. "I think you might know more than you let on."

A strange sensation twisted in Jo's stomach, a mix of unease and a sudden wave of dizziness. "What do you mean by that?" she pressed, trying to steady her voice.

Hazel's laugh was a dry cackle that seemed to echo in the cramped space. "You were there, weren't you?" she accused, her eyes glinting with a mix of cunning and madness.

Jo's instincts screamed that Hazel's grip on reality was tenuous at best. She might possess crucial information, but sifting truth from delusion appeared increasingly complex. Rising from her seat, Jo felt a wave of unsteadiness wash over her.

"Thank you for the tea, Hazel, but I really must go," she said, her words more rushed than she intended.

"But you're not leaving yet," Hazel protested with a sly smile. "I haven't gotten to the good part."

"I have to get back to the station," Jo insisted, her voice firm despite her spinning head. She moved toward the hallway, her steps cautious.

As she paused at the entrance of the dining room, curiosity tugged at her. She hesitated, her hand hovering near the doorframe.

"I wouldn't go in there, dear." Hazel's voice floated from behind, a warning laced with an unsettling undertone.

Jo stepped into the room.

CHAPTER THIRTY-THREE

Sam's eyes flicked to the empty space where the Crown Vic usually sat as he pulled into the station parking lot. Jo wasn't back yet? He felt a hint of concern as he let Lucy out and headed into the station. Lucy, trotting beside him, seemed to sense his unease, her ears perked and attentive.

As they entered the station, the smell of fresh paint greeted them. Reese, covered in a splatter of colors, was working on the hallway.

"Hey, Chief," Reese said.

"Hi. Have you seen Jo?" Sam asked, scanning the area.

"No." Reese stood, brushing a lock of hair from her face with her paint-streaked hand. "Haven't seen her since she left with you earlier today."

Sam shrugged and checked his phone. Jo must be on to something good.

They made their way into the squad room, Lucy's nails clicking gently against the linoleum. She paused and looked up at the top of the filing cabinet where Major perched. His brilliant green eyes bore into Lucy's with a mix of superiority and disdain.

Sam was about to continue on to his office when the door opened and Hank Madden wandered in, looking nervous. Interesting. Sam's instincts, honed by years of experience, told him that Hank had something big on his mind.

"Mr. Madden," Sam said. "What can I do for you?"

Hank's gaze darted around the room and finally back to Sam. "I thought a lot after you left, and I have some information.... about April."

"Shall we talk in my office?" Sam gestured toward his office, and Hank walked ahead. Sam followed him in and shut the door.

Sam took his place behind the desk while Hank settled into the chair in front, the uneven legs causing a slight wobble. Lucy took her spot near the window even though there wasn't much sun left to the day. The atmosphere was tense, the air thick with unspoken words.

Sam watched as Hank's gaze shifted uneasily to the corkboard adorned with the grim tableau of the crime scene. The widening of Hank's eyes betrayed his shock. "Is that where she was killed?" he asked, a tremor in his voice.

Sam responded with a simple nod, his keen eyes fixed on Hank, observing every nuance of his reaction.

Hank's gaze darted away from the corkboard, his throat bobbing with rapid, nervous swallows. The man's discomfort was almost palpable, filling the small office with a tense air. Sam waited patiently, his detective instincts kicking in. There was an authenticity to Hank's reaction that couldn't be easily feigned. Hank hadn't seen this crime scene before. He wasn't the killer.

"What did you want to tell me, Hank? Something you couldn't tell me before or something you just remembered?" Sam asked finally. His voice was calm but firm, cutting through the tense atmosphere.

Hank fidgeted in his seat, his eyes darting everywhere but at the corkboard. "I... uh, Danika doesn't know I'm here. She's at work," he stammered.

"I see." Sam smiled to urge Hank on.

Hank sighed. "The truth is I did meet with April the night she died. But she was alive when I left her, I swear."

Upon Hank's admission, Sam leaned forward, his demeanor calm yet assertive. "Why did you lie about meeting her, Hank?" he asked, his voice steady but laced with a hint of scrutiny.

Hank shifted uncomfortably in his seat, his hands fidgeting. "I was nervous," he confessed, his voice strained with emotion. "I didn't know what to say, and... and I didn't want Danika to find out I met with my ex. It's complicated."

Sam nodded slowly, understanding the human complexities of such situations. "I get that, Hank," he said, his tone softer but still firm. "But you have to see how it looks from our side. Lying about meeting April, especially under these circumstances, doesn't reflect well on you."

Hank's face crumpled, and he buried it in his hands, his body language exuding distress. "I know, I know," he muttered, his voice muffled and filled with regret. "That's why I came down to tell you the truth. I swear, she was very much alive when I left her. I wouldn't hurt her. I just couldn't."

Sam's next question was pointed. "Why did you meet her?"

Hank's discomfort was palpable. "I still have... had feelings for her. But she's changed. It was... disturbing."

Sam's gaze narrowed slightly as he assessed Hank's demeanor. "Disturbing enough to kill her?"

Hank's agitation spiked visibly. "No! I didn't kill her," he insisted, his voice rising in a mix of desperation and indignation. "Why would I come here to tell you I did meet her if I killed her?"

Sam remained calm, methodically piecing together the timeline. "Where did you meet her?"

"At that old diner outside of town," Hank replied, a hint of defensiveness in his tone.

"And what time was this meeting?" Sam continued, his questions deliberate.

"Nine p.m.," Hank answered.

"How long were you there with her?"

"Around forty minutes, give or take," Hank said, his gaze flickering away momentarily before returning to Sam.

"Where did she go after?" Sam asked.

Hank shrugged. "No idea. Said she had another meeting."

"That late at night?"

"That's what she said."

"And did you follow her?"

Hank shook his head vehemently. "No, I didn't follow her."

"What did you do?"

"I went to my friend's bar, O'Malley's in Lincoln. Stayed there, had a few too many and slept it off in his apartment above the bar."

Sam observed Hank's body language closely. The nervousness, the eagerness to provide details—it all painted a picture. But was it the truth?

"Seems odd then that Danika said you were at home with her all night," Sam said.

Hank chewed his bottom lip. "I know. I was surprised when she said that. I guess maybe she was trying to protect me. Or maybe she got the nights mixed up."

Sam remained silent.

After a few beats, Hank looked up at him. "Chief Mason, you have to believe me."

Sam nodded slowly. "Is there anything else you can tell me, anything that might help point to the killer?"

Hank thought for a few seconds then shook his head. "No. But you can check with my friend. His name is Bud O'Malley. He'll tell you I was there all night."

"Oh, don't worry, I will."

Hank stood. "Thanks, Chief."

As Hank left the office, Sam leaned back in his

chair, his thoughts swirling. Something about Hank's story didn't quite add up, but what? He picked up his phone, intending to message Jo for her take on it, but she hadn't replied to his last message. Where was she?

CHAPTER THIRTY-FOUR

J o stood frozen just inside the threshold of the dining room, her heartbeat kicking into overdrive at the figures she saw seated around the table. She drew her gun by instinct.

The room was dimly lit, casting elongated shadows across the table. The table was set for a tea party, complete with porcelain cups and saucers, each adorned with intricate floral patterns. A pot of tea sat in the center, steam gently rising from its spout. But it was the guests at this bizarre gathering that seized her attention with a jolt of eerie foreboding.

Looming around the table were giant stuffed animals, each dressed in human clothing. A bear, towering and imposing, wore a frilled blouse, its glassy eyes staring blankly ahead. Next to it, a bunny donned a flowered hat, its ears poking through the fabric. Jo's heart raced as she scanned the room, her initial alarm giving way to a surreal confusion.

She lowered her gun slowly, her gaze moving across the table. Each animal seemed more bizarre than the last. A stuffed dog wore a bow tie, looking almost comical with a tiny teacup placed before it. A moth-eaten fox in a waistcoat had its paw wrapped around a spoon as if poised to stir its tea.

Jo's mind reeled at the absurdity of the scene, her grip on the gun loosening. The air in the room felt thick, and a dizzying sense of disorientation washed over her. Her eyes traced the table settings, the untouched snacks, the half-filled cups, and the lifeless eyes of the plush guests.

Behind her, Hazel's voice cut through the eerie silence. "I told you not to go in there."

Jo turned sharply, her heart pounding in her chest. Hazel stood in the doorway, her eyes gleaming with a mix of mischief and madness. "What is this?" Jo managed to ask, her voice barely above a whisper.

Hazel chuckled softly, a sound that sent chills down Jo's spine. "It's my family," she said, her tone unsettlingly serene.

Jo's eyes returned to the table, and that was when she saw it. At the end of the table sat a large stuffed cat, its fur matted and dusty. But it was the shirt it wore that made Jo's blood run cold—sunshine yellow with white daisies, dirty and old, and unmistakably stained with blood. Tammy's shirt.

A gasp escaped Jo's lips as the realization hit her. Her arm felt impossibly heavy as she tried to raise her gun, her movements sluggish as if she were moving through thick mud. She turned back to Hazel.

"You?" she breathed, her voice laced with shock and horror.

Hazel's smile widened, revealing a set of crooked teeth. Her eyes sparkled with a sinister delight. "Yes, dear," she said, her voice dripping with a chilling satisfaction.

Jo's mind raced, her training kicking in despite the surreal circumstances. She needed to act, to arrest Hazel, to get out. But her body felt disconnected, her movements slow and uncoordinated.

As Hazel stepped closer, the room seemed to spin around Jo. The stuffed animals, the blood-stained shirt, Hazel's twisted smile—they all merged into a nightmarish tableau that threatened to engulf her.

She had to focus. She had to survive. But as Hazel's shadow loomed over her, Jo realized she might be too late. The truth was within reach, yet it felt more elusive and dangerous than ever.

CHAPTER THIRTY-FIVE

Kevin watched Bridget use her fork to cut a small piece of the lemon meringue pie she'd ordered. She looked up at him. "Thanks, by the way, for not telling anyone about that meeting outside of town."

Kevin shrugged, a half smile playing on his lips. "No problem. You kept my secret too." He sipped his coffee as Bridget chewed the bit of pie.

"How's your memory coming along?" Bridget's voice was soft, laced with genuine concern.

Kevin hesitated, his gaze drifting away momentarily. "It's fine," he said, though his voice lacked conviction. Inside, doubts gnawed at him. Was he really getting better? Memories seemed to come back in bits and pieces, like a puzzle he couldn't quite solve.

"I'm actually doing better, starting to remember things from before." His voice carried a hint of uncertainty, like he was trying to convince himself as much as Bridget.

As he placed the thumb drive on the table, Bridget's gaze followed the small device, her eyes reflecting a mixture of curiosity and concern. "What's that?"

He hesitated for a moment, the decision to share this with Bridget feeling more significant than he'd anticipated.

"This," he said, tapping the drive lightly, "is something I had in my bag from the hospital. At first I didn't know why, but then the other night I remembered that it had something to do with work."

Bridget's brow quirked up. "Really? And you had it since you were in the hospital? I hope it's not important."

"I don't think it is."

"What do you mean, you don't *think* it is?" Bridget forked more pie.

"Well, I don't remember exactly what it's for," Kevin said. "At first, I wasn't even sure it was police business. It was encrypted. But then I figured out how to look at the contents, and well... I don't see how it could be anything important."

"What's on it?"

Kevin paused then spoke. "It's just got pictures of some beech trees and some numbers," he began, watching her reaction closely.

At the mention of the beech trees, Bridget's eyes widened, her breath catching in her throat. "Beech trees?"

Kevin nodded, surprised at her reaction. "Yeah, is there some meaning to that?"

"Do they have markings on them?"

"Yeah, well, the branches at the bottom are broken in almost a pattern, and there is bark stripped from them. Not sure if that constitutes markings, but it doesn't look natural."

Bridget was practically jumping out of her seat. Maybe the thumb drive really was important? Judging by her reaction, it could be.

Bridget fished in her purse for a pen and grabbed a napkin from the table and started drawing. "Did they look like this?"

BRIDGET'S MIND raced as she turned the napkin to face Kevin. Her drawing was pretty basic, but she'd tried to depict the way the tree branches looked. This could be the missing piece, the link they had been searching for all along. But why did Kevin have this information, and what did it mean for them now? The questions multiplied, each one more pressing than the last.

He studied it. "Yeah, something like that."

Kevin's eyes flicked up from the napkin to meet hers. "How do you know about them?"

"We think those were made by a serial killer to mark where he buried his victims."

"What?" Kevin appeared shocked. "Who do you mean by *we*? What serial killer?"

Bridget sighed. "I guess I'd better start from the beginning."

As Bridget recounted the past, her heart weighed heavy. She locked eyes with Kevin across the table. "My sister Tammy was abducted when I was just five," she said, her voice soft but strained with enduring pain. That day's chaos and terror still haunted her.

"Our family fell apart after that," she continued, the raw ache in her voice evident. "That's what ultimately led to my spiral into addiction. I was seeking any escape from the relentless pain."

Kevin's face softened, and his hand found hers on

the table, offering comfort. She welcomed the soothing warmth.

"In contrast, Jo turned her grief into a quest for justice. She became a cop to find answers," Bridget said, her gaze momentarily drifting into distant memories.

"I'm so sorry. I never knew about that. Jo never said anything," Kevin said.

"Well, it's not something you bring up at a party." Bridget gave a sad laugh. "It's kind of hard to talk about."

"Of course," Kevin responded, his voice thick with empathy. "I hope they put the bastard away for good."

"That's the thing. They never caught him," Bridget replied, her voice tinged with bitterness. "But Jo's never given up. Now, Sam, Holden, and I are helping her."

"Helping her?" Kevin asked.

"Jo has been investigating this for years in her spare time. That's what led her to White Rock in the first place," Bridget said.

"What happened to the original case?"

Bridget shrugged. "Trail went cold, then it got put on the back burner. It hasn't been active in years. So we're working on it on our own."

Kevin's face showed a flicker of hurt. "I had no idea you all were working on this."

"Jo only recently brought everyone into the loop, even Sam. You were still in a coma back then. I'm sure they would've told you as soon as you were back to one hundred percent," Bridget quickly reassured him.

Kevin's expression softened with Bridget's words. "So you think these trees might be tied to the killer who took your sister?"

Bridget nodded, her eyes intense with a blend of hope and determination. "We haven't had much to go on, but there was a recent tip about our old babysitter moving to White Rock. It might all be connected. If her family was involved somehow..."

Her voice trailed off as she was caught in the labyrinth of possibilities. "If only we knew where those trees were," she added, frustration seeping into her tone.

Kevin thought for a moment, his brow furrowed in concentration. "There were also some numbers on the drive that I thought might be some sort of coordinates." He quickly pulled out his phone, fingers dancing over the screen as he entered the mysterious numbers.

The map zoomed into White Rock, pinpointing a location on Mountain Loop Road. Bridget's heart skipped a beat, adrenaline surging through her.

"What are we waiting for!" she exclaimed, leaping from her seat with a sudden burst of energy. Her eyes sparkled with a mix of excitement and resolve. This could be the breakthrough they'd been hoping for—a tangible lead in a case that had long seemed hopeless.

CHAPTER THIRTY-SIX

Sam sat alone in his office, the dim light casting long shadows across the room. He leaned back in his chair, his eyes fixed on the corkboard that covered an entire wall with photos and information about the April Summers case.

He mulled over his conversation with Hank Madden. The man's alibi had checked out, but something didn't sit right. Why had Danika lied to give Hank an alibi? Sam's gaze returned to the footprint. He had been so sure it belonged to Hank, but now doubts crept in. Could Hank's friend have lied for him?

A sudden commotion broke his concentration. "Lucy! No!" Reese's voice echoed from the reception area. A second later, Lucy bounded into Sam's office,

Major's new toy gripped firmly in her jaws. Close on her heels was Major, determined to reclaim his possession.

Sam leaned over the desk, watching the unfolding chaos. Lucy raced across the floor, leaving behind a trail of paint paw prints. Reese rushed in, rag in hand, frustration etched on her face. "They ran right through my trough of paint!"

Sam sprang into action, grabbing another rag to help clean up the mess. As he wiped, he noticed something odd about the prints. There was only one set, and they looked strange in the middle. He paused, realization dawning. The prints overlapped—Major had run through Lucy's exact footsteps.

A lightbulb went off in Sam's mind. He glanced back at the footprint on the corkboard, a surge of adrenaline shooting through him. The single set of footprints at the crime scene with the unusual tread— could they be overlapping prints too? Was it possible that two people were there when April was killed?

Sam had a suspicion of who those two people might have been. He tossed the rag back to Reese. "I gotta run!"

Reese looked up, surprised. "What? Sam, the mess!"

But Sam was already at the door, grabbing his

jacket. "Sorry, Reese! I'll explain later!" he called out as he dashed through the station.

Sam was halfway out the door when he heard the rapid patter of Lucy's paws behind him. The German shepherd was in full police mode, her playful demeanor replaced by a focused alertness. She seemed to understand they were on police business, her feud with Major momentarily forgotten.

As Lucy rushed past, the toy she'd been tussling over dropped from her mouth, landing with a soft thud on the floor. Major, close behind, stopped in his tracks. His bright, luminescent eyes widened in surprise as he sniffed at the abandoned toy. For a brief moment, he looked at Lucy, an expression of feline astonishment etched on his face. But then, as if deciding the toy was no longer of interest now that the game had ended, he turned and sauntered away with a dignified air.

Sam couldn't help but smile at the scene. It was clear to him that for Major, the joy was not in the toy itself but in the rivalry it sparked with Lucy. As he and Lucy made their way to the Tahoe, the dog left a partial paw print smudge of paint on the door. Sam noticed it but decided against cleaning it off. They were in too much of a hurry.

Sam whipped out his phone and sent a quick

message to Jo: *Might have a breakthrough. Heading to the logging site. Meet me there ASAP.*

He threw the car into gear and sped off. Every second counted. If his theory was correct, they were closer than ever to unraveling the mystery. But time was of the essence.

As Sam's car tore through the streets of White Rock, the setting sun cast a golden glow over the town. He just hoped he wasn't too late.

CHAPTER THIRTY-SEVEN

J o lay sprawled on the floor, her head spinning as she tried to focus on Hazel standing over her. "What did you do to me?" she managed to ask, her voice barely a whisper.

Hazel's laughter was chilling, echoing through the room. "Never accept tea from a stranger, dear," she taunted, her eyes gleaming with malice.

Jo's hand trembled as she reached for her gun, trying to lift it. But her muscles felt like they were made of jelly, unresponsive and weak. Hazel easily kicked the gun out of Jo's feeble grasp, sending it skittering across the wooden floor.

With surprising strength, Hazel hauled Jo up from the floor and forced her into one of the dining room chairs. Jo struggled, but her efforts were futile against Hazel's unexpected vigor. The old woman moved with a swift, unsettling agility as she secured Jo's wrists with zip ties.

Jo's heart raced as Hazel picked up the discarded gun, holding it with a familiarity that sent shivers down Jo's spine. The realization of her dire situation settled in, her mind racing for any solution, any chance of escape.

Hazel stepped back, studying Jo with a cold, calculating gaze. "You're in my world now, dear. And in my world, I make the rules."

Jo's mind raced, trying to piece together a plan amidst the fog that clouded her thoughts. She needed to stall, to find a way to alert Sam, to survive this nightmare. She'd made a fatal mistake and rushed out of Lily's without telling anyone. No one knew she was here.

Her eyes darted around the room, seeking anything that might help her. But all she found were the unnerving stares of the stuffed animals seated around the table, silent witnesses to her predicament.

"You don't remember me, do you?" Hazel's voice was taunting, a twisted smile curling her lips. "I visited the Duchamps—or should I say, the Woodsons—back then. Your family lived just down the street."

Jo's heart raced. Hazel had been to her childhood neighborhood? But her focus was on the gun, on Hazel's unstable demeanor. She needed to keep Hazel talking, to buy time, to find a way out of this.

"I don't remember you," Jo managed to say, her voice strained against the dryness of her throat.

Hazel chuckled, pacing around the table. "I saw Tammy then, such a perfect little thing. Easy to take. And there were others, many others. They're all out in the woods near the beech trees."

Jo's eyes flickered to the window. Outside was dense forest. Her breath caught in her throat. Was that where the answers to her sister's disappearance lay buried?

"What are you going to do with me?" Jo's voice was barely above a whisper, fear lacing her words.

Hazel leaned in close, her breath foul, her eyes wild. "Maybe it's time you joined your sister. Reunited at last."

She noticed Hazel's attention momentarily drift to the stuffed animals, a hint of madness in her gaze. Jo seized the moment, shifting in her chair, trying to wriggle her hands out of the zip ties. But Hazel's attention snapped back to Jo, her grip on the gun tightening.

"You're not going anywhere, dear," Hazel hissed, her finger twitching on the trigger.

Jo's heart pounded in her chest. She needed a miracle now, anything to turn the tide. She thought of Sam, of the investigation, of Bridget, of the years searching for Tammy. She couldn't let it end here, not like this.

CHAPTER THIRTY-EIGHT

The logging site felt eerily silent compared to the bustling activity of his last visit. The absence of chainsaws and machinery noises left the air almost unnaturally still, a stark contrast that heightened his senses.

Sam tapped his fingers on the steering wheel, glancing at his phone every few seconds. Jo should have been here by now. He knew she wouldn't want to miss this. If his theory was correct, this could blow the case wide open. He frowned at the empty message screen. It wasn't like Jo to be unresponsive.

Peering through the Tahoe's windshield, he noticed movement in the office trailer. Someone briefly peered out at his car before ducking away.

"They see us," he said to Lucy. "Guess we can't sit here and wait any longer."

With a sense of urgency, he grabbed his hat and stepped out of the vehicle. As he and Lucy made their way to the trailer, the door swung open, revealing Danika Madden's questioning gaze.

"What brings you here, Chief Mason?" Danika asked as she noticed Sam approaching the trailer.

Sam gave a nod, gesturing to the door. "Just a few more questions. Mind if I come in?"

Danika stepped back, opening the door wider to let him enter. Inside, Travis was seated at a makeshift desk cluttered with papers.

"Evening, Travis," Sam greeted casually.

Travis looked up, a hint of irritation in his eyes. "I told you everything the other day, Chief."

Sam smiled slightly. "Yeah, you know how it is. We have to dot every *i* and cross every *t*. Go over things several times. So, what are you doing here so late anyway?"

Danika and Travis exchanged a quick glance before Travis responded. "We're just going over the accounting. Like I told you before, it's a weekly thing, can't be done during the day since I'm busy with operations."

Sam nodded, making mental notes as he took in

their demeanor. "I see. Well, I won't take up too much of your time. Just need to clarify a few details about April Summers. You know, routine follow-up."

Danika nodded, her eyes darting from Sam to Travis. She fidgeted with a pen, trying to appear nonchalant.

Sam leaned against the edge of a cluttered desk. "You know, I'm curious about April Summers. She was quite vocal against your operation. Did that ever get... personal?"

Travis swallowed, his eyes flickering away. "Just business disagreements, nothing more."

Sam hummed thoughtfully. "You know, rumors say April had a knack for... let's say, persuasive tactics. Ever experience that?"

Travis shifted in his seat, a bead of sweat forming on his forehead. Danika stopped fidgeting, her grip tightening on the pen.

"Chief Mason," Danika started, her voice shaky. "We don't get involved in that sort of thing."

Sam's eyes narrowed slightly. "Speaking of involvement, Danika, why exactly did you provide Hank with an alibi? Was it for him or for yourself?"

The question hung heavily in the air. Travis's nervousness was palpable. He looked like a cornered animal. Danika's face paled, her mouth opening but no words coming out.

Sam pushed further, his tone more pointed. "We know April had a meeting that night shortly before she was killed. Someone who didn't want to be seen meeting with her. We figure she was trying to extort money."

Sam left plenty of room to make Travis sweat. If his theory was true, then Travis met with April at the owl sanctuary so no one would see them.

"Not surprising," Travis said.

Lucy sniffed the air, sensing the rising tension. Travis glanced at the dog, his resolve faltering.

"You know, plenty of people in town have Ring doorbells, and we're hoping to figure out who drove out on that road by looking at their recordings." It really wasn't true, but Sam figured the threat of it might get Travis talking. He was right.

Travis's eyes darted between Danika and Sam, a war of emotions playing out on his face. Sam's steady gaze finally broke through his defenses.

"Travis, we need the truth," Sam pressed. "What happened that night?"

Travis exhaled sharply, his shoulders slumping. "Okay. I did meet with April, but I swear, I didn't plan to kill her."

Sam leaned forward. "Go on."

Travis ran a hand through his hair, visibly grappling with the memory. "She said she'd stop the protests if I paid her. It was ruining the business, so I agreed to meet her. But I didn't want anyone to see us together, so she suggested the owl sanctuary."

Sam's eyes narrowed. "So you and Danika went out there together?"

Travis shook his head, avoiding Danika's gaze. "No, just me."

Sam sensed the inconsistencies but decided to keep Travis talking. "And what went wrong?"

Travis shrugged. "We argued over the price. She was asking for too much. She was... She was crazy, Chief. Then she pulled out a gun. We struggled, and it went off. I never meant for the owl to get hurt. It was an accident."

Sam studied Travis's face. "But you didn't shoot her? You used a log instead?"

Travis's eyes flickered to Danika, who now had tears streaming down her face. "I didn't club her."

Sam's gaze was unwavering, fixed on Danika. Her eyes, brimming with tears, conveyed a storm of emotions. "Tell me what happened, Danika," Sam urged gently, sensing the floodgates about to open.

Danika took a shaky breath, her voice trembling.

"I... I knew about Hank and April. I saw them in the diner and followed her afterward. To the owl sanctuary." She swallowed hard, a tear trailing down her cheek.

"And then?" Sam prompted her, his voice soft but insistent.

"I stayed hidden," Danika continued, her voice gaining a desperate pitch. "I saw Travis arrive, and they started arguing. It got heated... then April pulled a gun."

Sam leaned in, his focus intensifying. "What did you do?"

Danika's hands wrung together nervously. "I panicked. I couldn't let her shoot Travis. I picked up the nearest thing I could find—a log. I thought... I thought I'd just knock her out, stop her..."

Her voice cracked, and she paused, gathering herself. "But when I hit her, she... she fell onto that rock. It was horrible." Fresh tears streamed down her face.

Sam's expression softened slightly. He understood the weight of her unintended actions. "You didn't plan to kill her?"

Danika shook her head vehemently. "No, never! It was just a moment of madness. I wanted to protect Travis, to stop the madness."

"But then you wiped the gun clean, left the scene, and lied about being there."

Danika burst into tears.

Sam sighed deeply. "You understand I have to arrest you for this?"

Danika nodded, resigned. "I understand. I just... It was a split-second decision. I've regretted it every second since."

As Sam cuffed Danika, he glanced at Travis, whose face was etched with concern and guilt. "We'll need to talk more, Travis. There are still pieces to put together, and you lied as well."

"He didn't have anything to do with April's death," Danika said.

With Danika in custody, Sam led her outside, his mind heavy with the weight of her confession. Lucy followed, sensing the gravity of the situation, her demeanor serious. As they left, Sam's thoughts lingered on Jo's whereabouts. One mystery was closer to resolution, but another concern gnawed at him. Where in the world was Jo?

CHAPTER THIRTY-NINE

The drive into the heart of the woods on Mountain Loop Road felt like a descent into another world. Dense foliage and towering trees flanked the dirt road, creating a tunnel of shadows that swallowed Bridget and Kevin's car. Bridget sat rigidly in the passenger seat, her hands clenched tightly in her lap, while Kevin focused intently on the road, his eyes occasionally flicking to the GPS.

"This place feels... forgotten," Bridget murmured, gazing out at the darkening woods. Her breath fogged up the window, blurring the eerie landscape outside.

Kevin nodded, his jaw set. "Yeah, it's like we've stepped out of time." He slowed the car, peering ahead where the road seemed to dissolve into the encroaching wilderness.

The GPS beeped, indicating they had reached the vicinity of the coordinates. Kevin pulled the car onto the side of the dirt road, parking under the cover of a large oak tree. The engine's shutdown echoed eerily in the silence of the woods.

"We'll have to go on foot from here," Kevin said, his voice steady but with an undercurrent of tension.

Bridget nodded, her heart pounding in her chest. She grabbed the flashlight from the glove compartment, her fingers brushing against Kevin's as she did so. The brief contact was grounding, offering a moment of human connection amidst the fear and uncertainty.

They stepped out of the car, the doors closing with a thud that seemed too loud in the quiet of the forest. Bridget's flashlight cut a bright swath through the twilight as they ventured away from the road, guided only by the dim light and the GPS.

Every crunch of leaves underfoot sounded magnified, and the occasional rustle in the bushes sent jolts of fear through Bridget. Kevin led the way, his own flashlight moving methodically from side to side, scanning for any signs of the mysterious beech trees.

"Are you sure this is the right place?" Bridget whispered, her voice barely audible over the rustling leaves underfoot.

Kevin nodded, his eyes fixed on the GPS. "This is where the coordinates lead." Kevin turned to look around. "Right here."

Bridget scanned the tree trunks with her flashlight. "There," Bridget whispered, her voice barely audible. The beam of her flashlight revealed the distinct broken branches and the same stripped bark in the photo that Jo had. Of course, it looked a little different since so many years had passed. The trees had grown, but there was no mistaking those lower branches.

A cold shiver ran down Bridget's spine as she realized the significance of their discovery. This was it— the connection to her sister's disappearance. But their discovery was overshadowed by the ominous feeling of being watched, the woods around them holding secrets that were yet to be revealed.

As Kevin and Bridget crept through the dense underbrush, a faint glow caught Kevin's attention. "Wait, what's that?" he murmured, peering into the darkness.

Bridget followed his gaze, her eyes straining to make out the source of the light in the enveloping gloom of the forest. At first, it was just a dim, almost-imperceptible glimmer, but as they cautiously moved closer, the soft illumination gradually took shape.

"There's a house," Kevin whispered, disbelief

coloring his tone. The presence of any structure in this isolated part of the woods was unexpected, to say the least.

They moved closer, their footsteps muffled by the thick carpet of fallen leaves. The house, obscured by the trees, slowly came into view. It was an old farmhouse, its once-vibrant colors faded and peeling under the relentless assault of time and weather. The windows, dirty and cracked, emitted the faint light they had seen from afar, casting eerie shadows on the gnarled trees surrounding the house.

Kevin's attention was abruptly drawn to a familiar shape in the dim light. "Hold up," he whispered, squinting through the trees.

Bridget paused, following his gaze. There, parked in a clearing beside the old farmhouse, was the White Rock Police Department Crown Victoria sedan.

"Jo or Wyatt must be here. Sam always drives the Tahoe," Bridget breathed, a mix of relief and new anxiety coloring her voice.

Kevin nodded. "But why? This is too much of a coincidence. Something isn't right."

As they inched closer to the house, a chill ran down Bridget's spine. The silhouette of someone holding a gun in the window froze her in her tracks.

"Get down!" Kevin hissed, pulling her to the ground.

Kevin crept up to the side of the house, Bridget right behind him.

Bridget peered through the window, the sight that met her eyes sending her into a panic. It was Jo, her sister, tied to a chair, a gun pointed at her by an old woman.

Bridget's heart raced as she stared at the house, the shadowy figure with the gun visible through the window. Panic and determination warred within her. "We can't just stand here," she said, her voice barely above a whisper.

Kevin turned to her, his expression etched with concern. "Bridget, listen to me. You need to stay back. Go to the car and call Sam. I'm going in."

Bridget's eyes flashed with defiance. "And let you face that alone? No way. Jo's my sister."

"Bridget, it's too dangerous," Kevin insisted, the urgency in his voice rising. "You're not trained for this. We have no idea what we're walking into."

She set her jaw, her mind racing with memories of past dangers she'd faced. "I can't just hide while you go in there. I've faced worse, Kevin. I won't leave Jo."

Kevin's eyes softened for a moment, as if he understood her fear and resolve, but his tone remained firm.

"It's not about bravery. It's about being smart. I need you to be safe, and we need backup."

Bridget's heart pounded, her fear for Jo clashing with the realization of the risk. Reluctantly, she nodded, her voice tight. "Fine, I'll call Sam. But I'm not going far. And if you need me, I'm coming in."

Kevin hesitated then gave a curt nod, acknowledging her decision. "Just... be careful."

As Kevin moved stealthily toward the house, Bridget's resolve hardened. She couldn't just wait. She'd follow at a safe distance, ready to help. Her experience on the streets had taught her how to move quietly, how to survive. She wasn't about to run back to the car and risk losing the only sister she had left. With a deep breath, she crept forward, every sense alert.

CHAPTER FORTY

Jo still hadn't shown up by the time Sam was done booking Danika. Sam's anxiety spiked as Lucy paced restlessly by his side. The German shepherd's behavior sent warning signals flashing through his mind. Something was seriously wrong.

"Have you heard from Jo?" Sam asked Reese as she was on her way out the door.

Reese shook her head. "Not since earlier today. Is something wrong?"

"I'm not sure. She's not answering texts."

"The last time I saw her you guys had just come back from talking to Hank Madden." Reese stilled, her coat halfway on. "Do you need me to stay?"

"No. You go ahead home. I'm going to go check

with Lily Dunn. That's where Jo was going after our talk with Hank."

He drove quickly to Lily Dunn's art store and found her just as she was locking up for the night. The young artist looked surprised to see him. "Chief Mason? Is everything okay?"

"Lily, did Sergeant Harris come to talk to you?" Sam asked, his voice tense.

Lily's brow furrowed in confusion. "Yeah, earlier today. She came by asking about Ricky Webster."

Sam leaned in slightly, his instincts on high alert. "What exactly did you talk about?"

Lily, sensing the seriousness in his tone, took a deep breath. "Well, she came in asking about Ricky and his family." Her voice held a defensive edge.

Sam nodded, encouraging her to continue.

"She seemed really focused on his father and uncle," Lily said, fidgeting with the hem of her shirt. "Kept asking if they were in trouble a lot and stuff like that."

"And what did you tell her?" Sam pressed, watching her closely.

Lily shifted her weight from one foot to the other. "Not much because I don't really know anything about Ricky's family. I keep telling you guys that he's not a bad guy. What does it matter what his father or uncle did?"

Sam's gaze didn't waver. "Was there anything else?"

Lily started to shake her head, then her expression changed. "Yes, actually. She noticed my necklace." She instinctively reached up to touch the chain around her neck. "She seemed really interested in it."

Sam's focus sharpened. "What about the necklace interested her?"

"She started acting weird when she saw it. She practically grabbed it from my neck." Lily looked down at the crystal orb. "Asked where I got it."

"Where did you get it?"

"From Ricky. He said it was some kind of family heirloom." Lily stuck the key in the lock and locked the door. "As soon as I told her that, she rushed out. Kind of weird, if you ask me. Sorry I can't be more helpful."

"Actually, you've been more helpful than you know." Sam turned and rushed toward the Tahoe. Lucy was already in front of him, as if she knew what to do next.

"Weird," he heard Lily say as he rushed out. "That's exactly what Jo said."

As they drove, Lucy whined and shifted restlessly,

her behavior mirroring Sam's growing unease. The dog seemed to sense the urgency, her ears perking up, eyes focusing ahead as if she, too, was on a mission to find Jo.

Sam's thoughts raced as he pieced together the fragments. The necklace must have been physical evidence that connected Jo's sister to the Websters. Sam wasn't sure exactly what or how, but that had to be why Jo raced off. And if that was the case, then Jo had been at the Websters's house for hours. His grip tightened on the steering wheel, the fear for Jo's safety fueling his haste.

As the car sped through the darkening streets, Sam felt a growing sense of dread. He needed to find Jo—and fast.

CHAPTER FORTY-ONE

Kevin's hand rested on the latch to the screen door, his movements deliberate and cautious. The front door stood open, and he just needed to make it past the screen door without alerting anyone to his presence. He eased the door open, inch by painstaking inch, ensuring it remained silent. The hinge gave a faint protest, a whisper in the stillness that seemed magnified to his tense ears.

As the gap widened just enough to allow his entry, the dim interior of the house revealed itself. Shadows clung to the corners, stretching across the floor and up the walls, transforming mundane objects into sinister silhouettes. Every shape seemed to hold a threat, every darkened corner a potential danger.

Kevin paused, letting his eyes adjust to the gloom, his senses alert for any sound or movement, his heart pounding in his chest. Each step he took was calculated, his mind whirring with the training he thought he'd forgotten.

He could hear muffled voices from deeper within the house. Jo's tone was steady, but there was an underlying strain that sent a chill down Kevin's spine. Hazel's voice, on the other hand, was eerily calm, almost singsong.

Moving with deliberate slowness, Kevin assessed his surroundings. The hallway stretched before him, lined with framed pictures that gazed down like silent sentinels. He needed to get a sense of the layout, figure out where they were. The old wooden floorboards felt like treacherous terrain under his cautious steps.

A sudden creak from beneath his foot shattered the quiet. Hazel's voice sharpened. "What was that?"

Kevin froze. His mind raced.

The sound of a chair scraping against the wood floor came from the dining room, the noise oddly amplified in the stillness of the house.

Was that Jo? Did she know someone was here to help her so she was covering the noise? Or was it just a coincidence? Kevin couldn't afford to assume that Jo might be aware of his presence. He couldn't rely on her being in a position to assist him. In this moment, it was all on him.

Despite the gaps in his memory since the gunshot that had sent him to the hospital, Kevin felt a surge of confidence. His police training, deeply embedded in his psyche, hadn't failed him. For the first time since waking from his coma, Kevin felt a sense of capability and readiness. He was up to the task, relying solely on his own instincts and skills honed from years on the force. His memory, though fractured, served him well now.

Sweat beaded on his forehead as he crept forward. The realization that Jo was incapacitated gnawed at him. She wouldn't have let herself be overpowered and tied up if she'd been at full capacity.

Through a sliver of an open door, Kevin caught a glimpse of the dining room. He pulled back quickly, the bizarre scenario etched in his brain.

The table had been set for a tea party, but the guests were not what he expected. Large stuffed animals, adorned in an array of outlandish outfits, sat around the table. Each had a teacup placed meticulously in front of them, as if they were frozen in a moment of a genteel gathering.

Hazel's actions were more than just odd. They were the doings of someone deeply unhinged. Someone unpredictable.

At the center of this surreal assembly sat Jo, tied to a chair. Her head was drooping, but he could see her expression—a mixture of disbelief and resolve. Hazel held Jo's gun, her finger worryingly close to the trigger.

Kevin's mind raced. How could he overpower Hazel without getting shot? He had no weapon except maybe the element of surprise, but Hazel was bound to be unpredictable. He'd seen a doorway at the other end of the room. Hazel had her back to that door. If he could get around to that door, maybe he could signal Jo without Hazel noticing. They might have a chance if Jo's capacity to act hadn't been severely hindered.

He backtracked, his breath held tight in his chest. As he edged toward the other door, his mind played out the scenario. If Jo saw him, she'd know what to do. They had practiced this sort of silent communication in training sessions. One problem, though. Jo was tied to a chair and looked to be on the verge of falling unconscious.

Another problem. Hazel had a gun, and he didn't.

Surveying the interior, he saw a room at the end of the hallway. That room might offer both cover and a strategic view into the dining room. If Hazel remained oblivious to his presence, this could be his chance to signal Jo.

As he edged down the hall, Kevin paused to glance into the kitchen. The stillness assured him they were alone in this part of the house. He couldn't shake the urgency gripping him. At least Bridget was safe. Hopefully she'd called Sam and he was already on his way.

Every second mattered.

BRIDGET SHOULD HAVE CALLED Sam before following Kevin inside, but it was too late now. She kept to the shadowy area of the foyer, her footsteps light and controlled so no one would hear her. Her time on the streets had honed her ability to move unnoticed, a skill that now felt both familiar and unsettling. The dimly lit hallway stretched before her, each shadow a potential hiding spot, each creak a warning of her presence.

She glanced at Kevin's back, shrinking into the shadows as she watched him navigate the hallway with a focus that spoke of his own training. He was past the doorway to the room that Jo was held in and heading toward a room at the end of the hall. Bridget hesitated for a moment, torn between the urge to rush in and the knowledge that a single misstep could be disastrous.

Her mind raced with images of Jo tied to a chair, Hazel with a gun. She couldn't just stand there. She had to do something. But what? Calling Sam had been the sensible choice, and now she could kick herself for not doing as Kevin asked.

Her sister's voice sounded weak. "Why Tammy? Why did you have to take her?"

Hazel's laugh sounded like a cackle. "She was such a pretty little thing."

"She was only a child!" Jo's voice sounded stronger.

"I know." Hazel's answer was chilling.

"How did you pull it off?" Jo asked.

Hazel's confession seeped through the walls. She spoke of drugging Eve, the babysitter, to ensure she wouldn't interfere. The casual, almost-proud tone of her voice as she recounted how she had waited in the shadows, watching and waiting for her moment to snatch Tammy, sent shivers down Bridget's spine.

"It was easy to slip something into Eve's supper that night. Her mother had invited me to eat over." The ease with which she admitted this was staggering.

"How convenient," Jo answered.

Hazel's words were like poison. "I knew when Eve would be out, and I simply opened the door and walked in. I made it look like someone came in the window, though."

That explained a lot about the investigation and why the police had spent so much time on their father and Eve's family. She remembered some mumblings about it being someone the family knew, an inside job.

Bridget's breath hitched as Hazel continued. "Oh, Tammy did fuss. Thought she'd wake the whole house. Had to let her take that silly bauble necklace to keep her quiet."

Jo's voice, strained and hollow, asked the question Bridget dreaded to hear. "What... What did you do with her?"

Hazel's reply was cold and remorseless. "You don't really want to know, do you? It's not pleasant."

Bridget stifled a sob, her hand clamped over her mouth. The revelation was a physical blow, a vortex sucking the air from her lungs. Every moment of Hazel's confession was a torment, a twisted unveiling of the nightmare that had haunted their family for years.

Kevin's figure disappeared into the room at the end

of the hall, and Bridget detached herself from the shadows and crept over to the room on the right. It was a kitchen. She had an idea of what Kevin was planning. He'd maneuvered himself to surprise Hazel from behind. That might work great if he was the one with the gun, but Bridget knew he didn't have one.

She was going to have to provide backup somehow, and for that she'd need a weapon.

The kitchen was a mess of old dishes and clutter, but Bridget navigated it with ease, her eyes scanning for anything she could use as a weapon. She picked up a heavy frying pan, its weight reassuring in her hand. She was good using heavy objects as weapons. On the streets when you didn't have a gun or a knife, sometimes a heavy object was all you had.

She edged closer to the dining room, her heart thumping loudly in her ears. Every instinct screamed at her to be cautious, to be ready for anything. She could hear Jo's voice now, strained but steady, trying to keep Hazel talking.

Was Jo trying to distract Hazel because she knew they were here to help, or was she just buying time until someone came?

Bridget peeked around the corner, assessing the situation. Kevin was in position, ready to make his move. Hazel's back was partially turned, her focus on Jo.

This was it. Bridget tightened her grip on the frying pan, her body coiled like a spring. She knew the timing had to be precise.

So she got into position and waited.

JO SAT TIED to the chair, her mind swirling in a fog of confusion. The effects of the drugged tea Hazel had given her were evident in the dizziness and disorientation clouding her thoughts. She tried to focus, tried to make sense of the macabre stuffed animal tea party around her.

Keep her talking.

Jo managed to think up questions about her sister to keep Hazel distracted. To stop her from the next thing she had in mind. Sam would notice she was missing and figure out where she was. Sooner or later.

Unfortunately, she'd rushed off after she'd seen Lily with the necklace and had made the biggest mistake of her career. She hadn't told anyone where she was going. Maybe that wasn't the biggest mistake. Taking tea from a madwoman might have been the biggest.

Hazel moved around the room, her words a taunting melody of madness. She spoke in riddles and hinted at secrets from the past. Jo's heart raced with a mix of fear and a desperate need for answers. She strained against her bindings, seeking any slack, any hope of escape.

Her mind flashed back to her childhood memories —innocent days before Tammy's disappearance shattered their lives. Across the table, the stuffed animals, lifeless yet dressed for a party, seemed to mock her, their glassy eyes watching her struggle.

Was someone else here in the house?

She thought she had heard the creak of a floorboard earlier, and she'd tried to cover it up by wiggling her chair around. If it was Sam, she didn't want Hazel to investigate.

It seemed to have worked as Hazel remained focused on her. But no one had come barging in. If that noise had been Sam and Lucy, Jo was sure they'd be in here right now. Probably just the wind.

But then she saw it, a shadow in the hall!

Someone *was* here. But who?

Hopefully not Ricky, come to do his grandmother's evil bidding.

Jo forced herself to keep Hazel engaged. The key

was to keep her talking, to delay whatever end Hazel had planned.

"How many others, Hazel?" Jo asked, her voice steady despite the pounding of her heart.

Hazel let out a chilling laugh, a sound devoid of humanity. "Oh, many, dearie. So many." There was a twisted pride in her voice.

There it was, another shadow in the hall. As she tried to focus her blurry gaze past Hazel, she saw Kevin poke his head out. Their eyes met, a silent conversation passing between them in mere seconds. Jo gave a subtle nod, signaling her readiness. But was it only Kevin here? He didn't have his police gun. Would he be able to outmaneuver Hazel without a weapon?

She had to create a diversion.

Jo swallowed hard, pushing down the horror that threatened to overwhelm her. She subtly pulled the tablecloth, and the cup and saucer on it, toward her. "Did you have help with... all of this?"

Hazel's face contorted into a sneer, "Help? You think I needed help? No, I managed perfectly on my own. Much more efficient than that Joseph Menda." Her lips curled in disdain. "He's a pompous ass, if you ask me."

Menda was a known serial killer whom Jo had

interviewed once in prison. She agreed with Hazel that the guy was a pompous ass. "Did you work with him?"

Hazel's laugh echoed again in the cramped room. "Work with him? Please. I'm far more capable than he ever was."

Using her shoulder, Jo nudged the teacup. It shattered on the floor.

Hazel snapped her attention back to Jo, who looked down at the shards of the teacup.

"That was my grandmother's!" Hazel bent down to inspect the pieces.

Behind Hazel, Kevin quietly stepped into the room.

Jo, seizing the moment, threw her weight to one side, toppling her chair with a thud. She swung out her legs, aiming to kick Hazel to throw her off balance.

But Hazel reacted with alarming speed, the gun in her hand swiveling toward Kevin. Jo's heart skipped a beat as she saw Hazel's finger on the trigger.

Suddenly, in a blur of motion, a cast-iron frying pan soared through the air, striking Hazel in the chest with a resounding clang. The gun discharged, its deafening blast echoing through the room.

Jo, now sprawled on the floor, struggled to see the

aftermath. Her view was blocked, her heart racing with fear and uncertainty.

Had Kevin been hit? Where had that frying pan come from?

The tension was palpable, a heavy silence falling over the room as the dust began to settle.

CHAPTER FORTY-TWO

Sam and Lucy were halfway to the door of the farmhouse when he heard the gunshot. They took off at a run, bursting through the door, Sam with his gun at the ready.

The sound of the gunshot still echoed in his ears, setting his nerves on edge. Lucy's keen senses told her right where to go, and she didn't hesitate to run down the hallway into a room on the left. Sam followed.

He didn't know what he expected to see but certainly not this. The room was a bizarre tableau of giant stuffed animals seated at a table, their inanimate faces staring blankly. Stuffing floated through the air like snowflakes in a grotesque winter scene.

On the floor, Jo was sprawled, with Lucy hovering over her, frantically licking her face. Jo seemed shaken and dazed but unharmed. Bridget was cutting the zip ties that secured Jo to her chair.

Kevin was atop Hazel, pinning her to the ground. Hazel had a wild look in her eyes as she clutched a giant stuffed animal head that was rapidly losing its stuffing.

"You shot Bobby!" Hazel's voice was full of venom as she clutched the head, sounding close to tears.

"What happened here?" Sam scanned the room, taking in every detail, the strangest of which was a frying pan lying next to a smashed teacup.

He tried to piece together the events that might have led to this moment. He had no idea why Jo, Kevin, and Bridget would all be here, much less why they would be participating in this macabre tea party.

Jo rubbed her wrists where the zip ties had dug in and tried to steady herself with the help of Bridget. "Hazel is the one who took Tammy... and others."

Sam's brow quirked up. Hazel? Female serial killers were very rare, and he hated the idea that she'd been right here under his nose the whole time. "She confessed?"

Jo nodded, standing on shaky legs. "When I talked to Lily, she had this necklace on." Jo turned to Bridget. "It was mom's necklace, the one Tammy liked. It even had the chip where Tammy had dropped it in the driveway."

Bridget hugged Jo. "Maybe you shouldn't be talking." She turned to Sam. "Hazel drugged her tea."

Jo shook her head. "No, it's okay. I need to explain. When I saw that necklace, I rushed here without thinking."

Sam nodded. It was starting to make more sense. "When you never answered my texts or showed up back at the station, I went to Lily's, and she told me you rushed out after finding out Ricky had given her that necklace."

Jo looked apologetic. "I should've let you know, Sam. I had no idea it would turn out like this." She gestured to the bizarre scene around them. "She drugged me and took my gun."

Meanwhile, Hazel continued her struggle, her eyes wild. "Bobby made me do it! I did nothing wrong!" she shrieked, her voice cracking as Kevin finally clicked the handcuffs around her wrists.

Sam's focus shifted to Kevin. "Good job, Kevin. But how in the world did you know to come here?"

Kevin shifted uneasily. His voice was steady, but his hands betrayed a slight tremor as he told Sam about discovering the contents of the thumb drive. "I was actually on my way to give it to you." He paused, his gaze flickering to Bridget. "I stopped at the diner for a coffee... and ran into Bridget there. We got talking."

Bridget nodded as if to lend credence to his story.

"The thing is," Kevin continued, "I didn't even remember why I had the thumb drive. It was just there, with my stuff from the hospital. But then Bridget mentioned something about her sister and the beech trees, and I realized the numbers on the drive were actually coordinates."

Kevin glanced at Jo, an apologetic edge to his tone. "If I had known the significance, I would have brought the drive to you sooner, Jo. I'm sorry."

Jo, her expression softening, shook her head slightly. "No need to apologize, Kevin. You would have no way of knowing about any of that. I was going to bring you in on this, too, but I didn't want to over-whelm you."

"It's fine," Kevin assured her. "Anyway, the coordi-nates on the drive pointed to the woods out back here. We had to see if it led to the beech trees related to Tammy's case."

Jo glanced at Bridget. "And did they?"

Bridget nodded. "There's a stand of beech trees out back in the woods with lower branches broken and stripped of bark long ago. We saw the lights on in the place through the trees and came to investigate then saw you inside."

"I came in to distract Hazel and hopefully get your gun from her," Kevin said.

"Thanks for that. You did good." Jo smiled at Kevin then turned to Bridget. "But what are *you* doing in here?"

Bridget looked sheepish. "I followed Kevin in. He told me to go back to the car and call Sam, but I... Well, I didn't."

Sam's attention was drawn to the frying pan on the floor. "And the frying pan?"

Bridget grimaced. "I thought it might make a good weapon."

Kevin chimed in. "Turns out she was right. If that pan hadn't hit Hazel and thrown off her aim, she would have shot me instead of Bobby."

With a firm grip, Kevin hauled Hazel, who had been muttering and crying the whole time, to her feet. Jo leaned on Bridget as they all made their way out of the house.

"Hazel's confession makes things a lot easier," Sam said.

Suddenly the old woman straightened up and glared at Sam. "I didn't confess to anything!"

Kevin gripped her arm tighter. "Yes, you did. Jo heard you, and so did I."

"That was Mitzi talking!" Hazel pointed to the bunny with the flower hat.

Sam wondered if she was laying the groundwork for an insanity defense. "You can tell us more about Mitzi down at the station."

"Just don't blame Ricky. He's a good boy. Tell him I'll be home soon," Hazel said as she shuffled alongside Kevin.

As they walked out, Sam took Jo's arm since she was still a bit shaky. Lucy pressed against her leg, her way of lending support.

"This will be the second person I've booked today," Sam said.

Jo looked at him in surprise. "Second?"

"Yeah," Sam replied. "I solved the April Summers case while you were out here drinking tea. I'll tell you all about it after you get checked out at the hospital. We need to make sure Hazel didn't give you anything too damaging."

CHAPTER FORTY-THREE

T hree days later...

THE WARM GLOW of the firepit flickered across the faces of those gathered in Jo's backyard, casting a soft light on the close-knit group. It was a serene fall evening, a gentle breeze carrying the scent of burning wood and fresh pie.

The fire crackled and popped as Sam tossed another log onto the flames, sending a flurry of sparks dancing into the night sky.

Mick, relaxed and contemplative, sat on a tree stump, his legs crossed at the ankles. In one hand, he held a cup of something dark and strong, his other hand balancing a paper plate.

Jo, comfortably nestled in her camping chair, cradled a mug as the steam wafted up, mingling with the crisp night air. She took a careful sip, savoring the warmth and sweetness of the pumpkin chai.

Kevin, perched casually atop the cooler, had become Lucy's new best friend for the evening. The German shepherd sat obediently beside him, her eyes following every bite of pie that moved from the plate to Kevin's mouth. Occasionally, some pie made it to her own mouth.

Holden, meanwhile, lounged in a lawn chair, his posture relaxed but his eyes keenly observing the group. His drink, a modest glass of amber liquid, rested on the grass beside him within easy reach.

Bridget had laid out an array of homemade pies, a taste test of sorts before she baked one for Jo to bring to their landlord. She watched, amused, as her companions debated which pie might win over the old man's heart.

"So, which one are we thinking for Garvin?" Jo asked, her voice warm and light. She took a bite of the apple pie, the cinnamon and apple flavors bursting on her tongue.

"I bet he's an apple pie kinda guy," Mick chimed in, holding up his slice for emphasis. "Classic, reliable, can't go wrong with it."

Kevin, delicately balancing a piece of cherry pie on his fork, disagreed. "I don't know. This cherry pie is something else. It's got that perfect balance of tart and sweet. Might be a nice surprise for him."

Holden, thoughtfully sampling the pumpkin pie, weighed in. "There's something to be said for the subtlety of this pumpkin pie, though. It's not overly sweet, just right for a fall evening."

Bridget laughed, delighted at their debate. "I'm glad you all like them. I was thinking the pecan pie might be his favorite. It's rich and a bit different."

Lucy, sitting loyally beside Kevin, looked up expectantly as he fed her another small piece of pie crust. She seemed to agree with whatever choice would result in more treats for her.

Sam, who had been quietly enjoying each sample, finally spoke up. "Well, I think Garvin will be happy with any of them. But, if we're placing bets, my money's on the apple pie. It's a safe bet for winning someone over."

Suddenly, Lucy, ever alert, pricked up her ears and turned her gaze toward the edge of the woods.

Everyone followed her gaze to see Pickles, the little orange cat, hesitantly peeking out from the shadows.

"Aww, he looks scared," Bridget observed softly, noting the cat's apprehension amidst the unfamiliar crowd.

Jo smiled, watching the feline with a mix of concern and affection. "Not used to all the people here, I guess."

For a moment, Pickles seemed to weigh his options, cautiously taking a step forward toward the warmth and light of the fire. The group stilled, silently encouraging the cat to join them. However, as Lucy shifted slightly, sitting up with interest, Pickles seemed to make up his mind.

With one swift movement, the cat turned and disappeared back into the safety of the woods. Jo sighed, a hint of disappointment in her voice. "Hopefully, he'll come back later."

Sam chuckled, tossing another log onto the fire. "Don't worry, he knows where the good food is. I'm sure he won't stray too far."

Holden, gazing into the fire, spoke in a more somber tone. "FBI's gonna start digging up the woods behind Hazel's house."

Jo's eyes clouded with a mix of emotions. The idea

of finding closure was comforting, yet the image of Tammy's bones, hidden in the dirt for so long, unsettled her stomach.

Sam, sensing her discomfort, added gently, "With Hazel's confessions, there might be a lot of digging. She's been cagy about the exact numbers, but it could be dozens."

Jo shivered, despite the warmth of the fire. "Matching those bones to cold cases... some of them decades old... That's a daunting task."

"Yeah," Mick chimed in, "but at least Ricky's cooperating. Gave the FBI permission to search the woods. Maybe the kid isn't as bad as everyone thought."

Jo nodded slowly, a thoughtful look crossing her face. "At least Hazel only gave me a sedative in that tea," she said, trying to lighten the mood.

Sam raised his beer to her. "I'm glad. I can't afford to lose my second in command." He chuckled, earning a playful eye roll from Jo. "Though now that Kevin is back full time..."

"I'm sure I couldn't replace Jo," Kevin joked, raising his beer to Jo.

"I'm so glad you're back. We can use the help," Jo said.

"I just hope I don't disappoint. I am glad to have

my gun back, though. Could have used that at Hazel's," Kevin said.

"You proved you're more than capable," Sam said, clinking his bottle against Kevin's. "Doctor couldn't argue after that rescue."

"I'll second that," Jo said. "Weird that Wyatt didn't find anything else on that thumb drive." They'd given the drive to Wyatt, figuring that if more was hidden on there he'd be able to uncover it, but there was nothing else.

"Nothing else on it but those trees and coordinates," Sam mused, looking at Kevin. "Still a mystery where it came from."

Kevin shook his head, his expression a mix of frustration and acceptance. "I wish I could remember."

Jo scrunched up her face. "It's odd because that means that someone knew about this and put it on that thumb drive, and somehow Kevin ended up with it. But who gave it to him and why?"

Kevin shook his head. "I have no idea. Could it have been part of an investigation that somehow ended up in my pocket when we got that call?"

Sam shook his head. "If it was, I would think one of us would know about it too."

"Maybe you found it at the station? We found pictures of the beech trees in Tyler's things, and I suppose he could have had a thumb drive tucked away around there. You might have found it and not had a chance to mention you had it," Sam said to Kevin.

"If it was Tyler's, then we might never know why he had it." Jo shrugged as if accepting the fact then turned to Sam. "What's going on with the April Summers case?"

"Danika is being charged with involuntary manslaughter," he explained. "And Travis as an accomplice. If only they'd called the police..."

"It really was an accident," Kevin added. "But hiding it made things worse."

"At least those owl protesters are gone. Satisfied the 'owl killer' was caught," Jo said.

"Bet Jamison is happy about that." Holden poked at the fire with a stick.

"Can't wait to see how this mayoral election turns out," Mick said with a hint of disdain in his voice. "I saw a campaign commercial from that Marnie Wilson person. Don't know who's worse, her or Jamison."

The group shared a collective groan, the future of the town hanging in the balance of the upcoming election.

Sam stared into the fire, the flames reflecting in his eyes. "Well, things are bound to get heated on the campaign trail," he said, his voice carrying a note of foreboding. "Let's just hope it doesn't turn deadly."

****

WHO IS SAM KIDDING, of course it turns deadly. Find out who, how and why in book 8, Breaking Rules.

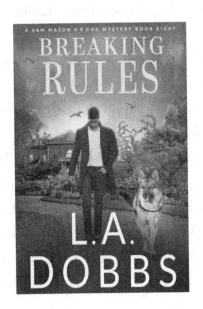

Sam Mason Mysteries

***

Telling Lies (Book 1)

Keeping Secrets (Book 2)

Exposing Truths (Book 3)

Betraying Trust (Book 4)

Killing Dreams (Book 5)

Crossing Lines (Book 6)

Seeking Justice (Book 7)

Breaking Rules (Book 8)

More books in the Rockford Security Series:

One Lie Too Many

Blink Of An Eye

Cold As Her Heart

A Game of Kill

No One To Trust

No Time To Run

Don't Fear The Truth

Hide From The Past

Liars Island Suspense Novellas:

***

Liars Lane

ABOUT THE AUTHOR

L. A. Dobbs also writes light mysteries as USA Today Bestselling author Leighann Dobbs. Lee has had a passion for reading since she was old enough to hold a book, but she didn't put pen to paper until much later in life. After a twenty-year career as a software engineer, she realized you can't make a living reading books, so she tried her hand at writing them and discovered she had a passion for that, too! She lives in New Hampshire with her husband, Bruce, their trusty Chihuahua mix, Mojo, and beautiful rescue cat, Kitty.

Her book "Dead Wrong" won the "Best Mystery Romance" award at the 2014 Indie Romance Convention.

Her book "Ghostly Paws" was the 2015 Chanticleer Mystery & Mayhem First Place category winner in the Animal Mystery category.

Join her VIP Readers group on Facebook:
    https://www.facebook.com/groups/ldobbsreaders

Find out about her L. A. Dobbs Mysteries at:
http://www.ladobbs.com

Made in the USA
Monee, IL
14 January 2025

76832329R00184